EASTER EGG THEFT

Jim and Ginger Cozy Mysteries Book 7

Arthur Pearce

Copyright © 2025 Arthur Pearce

All rights reserved.

No part of this book may be reproduced, distributed, or transmitted in any form or by any means, including photocopying, recording, or other electronic or mechanical methods, without the prior written permission of the author, except in the case of brief quotations embodied in critical reviews and certain other noncommercial uses permitted by copyright law. For permission requests, please contact the author.

"Easter Egg Theft" is a work of fiction. Names, characters, businesses, places, events and incidents either are products of the author's imagination or are used fictitiously. Any resemblance to actual persons, living or dead, events, or locales is entirely coincidental.

ISBN: 979-8-3136-5042-5

Contents

Chapter 1	1
Chapter 2	13
Chapter 3	27
Chapter 4	41
Chapter 5	53
Chapter 6	67
Chapter 7	79
Chapter 8	93
Chapter 9	103
Chapter 10	117
Chapter 11	129
Chapter 12	139
Chapter 13	149
Chapter 14	159

Chapter 15	169
Chapter 16	181
Chapter 17	195
Chapter 18	209
Chapter 19	221
Chapter 20	233
Jim and Ginger's Next Case	247
Bonus Content	249
Jim and Ginger's First Case	251

Chapter 1

The persistent tapping on my forehead pulled me from the depths of sleep. I cracked open one eye, immediately regretting it as the dim morning light assaulted my vision. Ginger's face hovered inches from mine, his green eyes narrowed with determination.

"Rise and shine, old man," he meowed, punctuating each word with another tap of his paw. "The early bird catches the worm, and all that nonsense."

I groaned, rolling over to squint at the alarm clock on my nightstand. The glowing red numbers mocked me: 7:00 AM. "Ginger," I mumbled into my pillow, "it's ungodly early. Go back to sleep."

"Ungodly early?" Ginger scoffed, leaping onto my back with enough force to knock the wind out of me. "It's the perfect time to start our day. Just enough time for a run, a shower, and then off to the Easter Fair. You wouldn't want to miss all the excitement, would you?"

I lifted my head just enough to glare at him. "The Fair doesn't start until ten. We have plenty of time."

Ginger kneaded my back, his claws pricking through the thin fabric of my t-shirt. "Ah, but you're forgetting something crucial, my dear Watson. It's April now. Warm weather. Ring any bells?"

With a sinking feeling, I recalled the promise I'd made months ago, back when the chill of winter had made it easy to postpone exercise. "I'll start running again when it's warm," I'd said, feeling very noble at the time. Now, faced with the reality of that promise, I was regretting my moment of fitness-inspired bravado.

"Five more minutes," I pleaded, burrowing deeper into my blankets.

Ginger was having none of it. He marched up to my head, his tail swishing back and forth across my face. "Oh no, you don't. We had a deal, Jim. Besides, after months of hibernation, you need all the time you can get to wheeze your way around the block."

With a heavy sigh that seemed to come from the very depths of my soul, I hauled myself into a sitting position. "Fine, you win. But coffee first."

Ginger's eyes widened in horror. "Are you insane? Coffee before running? Do you want to end up puking in Mrs. Henderson's prized petunias? Or worse, have a heart attack right there on the sidewalk? Although," he added thoughtfully, "that might finally give her something legitimate to spy on."

"Alright, alright," I grumbled, swinging my legs over the side of the bed. "No coffee. But don't blame me if I'm even grumpier than usual."

I shuffled over to the closet, rummaging around for my long-neglected running clothes. After several minutes of searching and a string of muttered curses, I finally located a faded t-shirt and a pair of shorts that had seen better days. As I struggled to pull them on, I became acutely aware of just how much I'd let myself go over the cold months.

The shorts, once loose, now clung desperately to my waist. The t-shirt stretched ominously across my midsection, threatening to split at the seams. I caught sight of myself in the mirror and winced. I looked less like a detective and more like an overstuffed sausage playing dress-up.

Ginger, perched on the dresser, tilted his head to one side. "Well," he said, in a tone that was far too cheerful for the occasion, "I see you've been taking fitness tips from Sheriff Miller. Tell me, Jim, are you trying to outdo his donut-enhanced physique?"

I shot him a withering glare. "Keep it up, furball, and I'll trade you in for a goldfish. They're much quieter in the mornings."

"Ah, but can a goldfish help you solve crimes?" Ginger retorted, leaping down to weave between my legs. "Besides, you'd miss my charming personality."

"Charming isn't the word I'd use," I muttered, but there was no real heat in it. Despite his early morning tyranny, I knew I'd be lost without Ginger. He'd become more than just a partner in our detective agency; he was a friend, companion, and, apparently, my personal trainer.

We made our way toward the front door, Ginger bounding ahead while I followed at a more sedate pace, my joints creaking in protest with each step. As I reached for the door, a thought struck me.

"Wait," I said, "don't I need to stretch or something?"

Ginger looked up at me, his expression a mixture of amusement and exasperation. "Jim, at this point, just making it to the end of the driveway without collapsing will be a stretch. We'll start small. Baby steps."

With a deep breath that did little to settle my nerves, I opened the door and stepped out into the mild morning air. The sun was just beginning to peek over the horizon, painting the sky in soft hues of pink and gold. In any other circumstance, I might have appreciated the beauty of the moment. However, my focus was entirely on trying to remember how legs worked.

We set off down the street at what could generously be called a jog. It was more of a fast shuffle, really, but I was moving and that seemed like a victory in itself. Ginger trotted alongside me, occasionally darting ahead and then circling back, like a sheepdog herding a particularly slow and uncooperative sheep.

We'd barely made it to the end of our street when I heard a familiar voice call out, "Well, well! Look who's decided to join the land of the living!"

I glanced over, my already labored breathing hitching slightly as I spotted Mrs. Henderson on her porch. She was settled into her usual chair, a pair of binoculars dangling around her neck and a mug of what I assumed was coffee clutched in her hands. Her eyes twinkled with mischief as she surveyed my red-faced, wheezing form.

"Good morning, Mrs. Henderson," I managed to gasp out between breaths. "Lovely day for a run, isn't it?"

She cackled, a sound that reminded me of a gleeful witch. "Oh, indeed it is! I have to say, Mr. Butterfield, you look like you're one step away from needing CPR. Should I have my finger ready to dial 911?"

I forced a smile, which probably looked more like a grimace. "No need for that. I'm as fit as a fiddle."

"A fiddle that's been left out in the rain, maybe," Ginger muttered, just loud enough for me to hear.

Mrs. Henderson leaned forward, her eyes narrowing as she studied me. "You know, all joking aside, it is good to see you taking care of yourself. Much better for your health than, say, sitting on a porch and watching for mysterious minivans."

I couldn't help but chuckle at that. "Well, we all have our callings, Mrs. Henderson. Someone has to keep an eye on the neighborhood, after all. Heaven knows our police force isn't up to the task."

She nodded sagely, raising her mug in a mock salute. "Truer words were never spoken, Mr. Butterfield. You keep running, and I'll keep watch. Between the two of us, we'll keep this town safe and fit!"

With a final wave, I continued on my way, Ginger trotting ahead. As we turned the corner, I heard Mrs. Henderson call out one last piece of advice: "Don't forget to breathe, Mr. Butterfield! It's rather essential to this whole 'staying alive' business!"

We made our way through the quiet streets of Oceanview Cove, the town still mostly asleep at this early hour. The only sounds were the slap of my running shoes against the pavement, my increasingly labored breathing, and Ginger's occasional encouraging (or sarcastic) meows.

As we passed the local elementary school, I noticed a group of teachers decorating the fence with colorful Easter-themed cutouts. Miss Chambers, the biology teacher who had recovered remarkably well from her former student Liam's death a few months ago, waved cheerfully as we passed. "Looking good, Mr. Butterfield!" she called out. I managed a weak wave in return, wondering if she needed her eyes checked.

We rounded another corner, and I nearly collided with Mr. Fenton, the town's most enthusiastic jogger. Despite being well into his seventies, Mr. Fenton ran every morning without fail, rain or shine. He barely broke stride as he passed us, calling out a chipper, "Beautiful morning for a run, isn't it?" as he disappeared around the next corner.

"Did you see that?" I wheezed to Ginger. "He's several years older than me and running circles around us."

Ginger looked up at me, his whiskers twitching with amusement. "Well, Jim, some people age like fine wine. You, on the other hand, seem to be aging more like milk left out in the sun."

As we approached the town square, I was surprised to see it already bustling with activity. Colorful tents were being erected, their canvas flapping in the morning breeze. The smell of fresh paint mingled with the salty sea air as last-minute touch-ups were applied to various stalls and booths.

"Looks like they're getting an early start on the Easter Fair," I panted, grateful for any excuse to slow down.

Ginger circled around me, his tail swishing with impatience. "Yes, yes, very interesting. Now keep moving, old man. You're not fooling anyone with this 'casual observation' act."

I grumbled but picked up the pace again, my legs feeling like they were made of lead. We skirted around the edge of the square, dodging workers carrying boxes of decorations and baskets overflowing with plastic eggs. A group of volunteers was setting up a stage for what looked like an Easter play, complete with oversized bunny costumes and a cartoonishly large carrot prop.

As we passed Emma's fortune-telling tent, I caught a glimpse of her inside, arranging her crystals with meticulous care. She looked up as we passed, her eyes widening in surprise.

"Jim!" she called out, waving enthusiastically. "The stars didn't foretell this! What a wonderful surprise!"

I raised a hand in greeting, not daring to stop for fear that I might never start again. "Morning, Emma," I wheezed. "Just... getting some exercise."

She beamed at me, her numerous necklaces clinking as she moved. "Oh, how marvelous! You know, I have a crystal that's excellent for stamina. Perhaps you'd like to-"

"No time!" I gasped, picking up speed. "Maybe later!"

As we left the square behind, Ginger looked up at me with what I swore was a smirk. "Stamina crystal? Might not be a bad idea, considering your current state."

"Very funny," I grumbled. "I'm doing just fine."

We continued our run, if you could call it that, heading toward the harbor. The familiar sight of boats bobbing gently in the water came into view, and I felt a surge of relief. Surely we'd gone far enough by now?

As if reading my mind, Ginger spoke up. "Don't even think about it, Jim. We're only halfway through our route."

I groaned, my legs protesting with every step. "You're enjoying this, aren't you?"

"Immensely," Ginger purred. "It's not every day I get to watch a human impersonate a wheezing locomotive."

As we approached the docks, I spotted a familiar figure preparing his boat.

"Robert!" I called out, waving as we approached. "Good morning!"

Robert looked up, his bushy eyebrows rising in surprise as he took in my disheveled, sweaty appearance. "Well, I'll be," he said, a smile tugging at the corners of his mouth. "If it isn't our local Sherlock Holmes, out for a morning stroll. Trying to outrun the ghosts of cases past, Jim?"

I chuckled, bracing my hands on my knees as I tried to catch my breath. "Not... not today. Just trying to... stay in shape."

Robert's eyes twinkled with amusement. "Is that what you call this? Well, I suppose movement of any kind counts as exercise these days."

Ginger let out a meow that sounded suspiciously like a laugh. I shot him a glare before turning back to Robert. "Very funny. I'll have you know I'm making excellent progress." I straightened up, trying to muster what was left of my dignity. "So, heading out to sea?"

Robert nodded, his expression turning more serious. "Aye, that I should. Got an order to fill today. There's a storm brewing for tomorrow, so it's now or never."

"A storm?" I asked, frowning. "But what about the Easter Fair? Surely you're not going to miss it?"

Robert shook his head. "Afraid I'll have to sit this one out. But Olivia and Leo will be there. The boy's been talking about nothing else for weeks. Seems there's some sort of Easter Egg Hunt he's determined to win."

I nodded, remembering Shawn mentioning the game after our last case. "I'll keep an eye out for them. And good luck with the fishing."

Robert grinned, gesturing at my sweat-soaked shirt. "Thanks, Jim. Though it looks like you're the one who needs the luck. Maybe take it easy on the way back? That shade of red isn't natural on a human face."

As we said our goodbyes and continued on our way, I said to Ginger, "See? Even Robert thinks I should take it easy."

Ginger, however, seemed unmoved. "Robert isn't your personal trainer, is he? No, that dubious honor falls to me. Now, less talking, more running. We've got a long way to go before you're back in fighting shape."

With a groan that seemed to originate from my very bones, I picked up the pace again. We made our way back through town, passing by Sophie's bakery. Through the window, I could see Sophie and Alice hard at work, likely preparing treats for the Fair. They looked up as we passed, offering friendly waves that quickly turned to concerned looks as they took in my bedraggled state.

"Do I really look that bad?" I muttered to Ginger as we rounded the corner.

"Let's just say if this detective thing doesn't work out, you have a promising career as a before picture in fitness advertisements," Ginger replied cheerfully.

As we finally turned onto our street, I felt a surge of relief. Home was in sight, and with it, the promise of a shower and a well-deserved rest. Mrs. Henderson's porch was surprisingly empty as we passed.

"Well, well," I panted, "looks like Mrs. Henderson has abandoned her post."

"Perhaps she's preparing for the Fair," Ginger suggested. "I heard she has her own tent this year. No doubt a hub for all the latest town gossip and mysterious minivan sightings."

As we approached our house, my eyes were drawn to a familiar car parked in front of the B&B. Before I could comment on it, the car doors opened, and two figures stepped out.

I blinked, sure that my oxygen-deprived brain was playing tricks on me. But no, there was no mistaking those familiar faces.

"Is that..." I began, my tired legs finally grinding to a halt.

Ginger finished my thought, his tail swishing with interest. "Lily and Aaron? Indeed it is. Well, well, it seems our little seaside town is in for some excitement after all."

Chapter 2

As Lily and Aaron approached, I couldn't help but marvel at how much Lily had grown since I'd last seen her. At sixteen, she was noticeably taller, her long brown hair pulled back in a messy bun that somehow managed to look both careless and stylish. Despite the changes, her light blue and pink backpack remained the same, a familiar anchor to the girl I remembered.

Aaron looked different too – the worry lines that had creased his face during our last encounter had softened, giving him a more youthful appearance. The anxious father I'd met during Lily's disappearance had been replaced by a more relaxed, easy-going version of himself.

"Mr. Butterfield! Ginger!" Lily called out, her face lighting up with a bright smile.

I chuckled, still trying to catch my breath from our run. "Well, what a surprise! What brings you two back to Oceanview Cove?"

Aaron grinned, clapping me on the shoulder. "We wanted to make it a surprise. Lily's on holiday, and we thought it'd be nice to visit for the Easter Fair and catch up with old friends."

Lily crouched down, reaching out to pat Ginger. To my amusement, he seemed pleased by the attention, arching into her hand with a contented purr. "I can't believe you're still running," Lily said, looking up at me with a mixture of admiration and skepticism. "I remember you were doing this the first time we visited, too."

I shifted uncomfortably, acutely aware of how my sweat-soaked shirt clung to my body and the way my shorts seemed determined to cut off circulation to my lower half. "Ah, well... I took a bit of time off from the whole fitness thing. Just getting back into the swing of it now."

"And by 'a bit of time off,' he means he's been hibernating like a particularly lazy bear," Ginger meowed, though of course, only I could understand him. "It's a miracle he made it this far without collapsing."

Eager to change the subject, I cleared my throat. "So, Lily, how's school going?"

Lily's eyes lit up. "It's going great! I just finished a big history project on the American Revolution. Got an A+ and everything. Oh, and I joined the debate team this year. We made it to regionals!"

As Lily spoke, noticed how animated she became, her hands moving expressively as she described a particularly heated debate about climate change. It was a far cry from the shy, reserved girl we'd met last year.

"That's fantastic," I said, genuinely impressed. "I hope all this success means you won't be going on any more treasure hunts, though. I don't think my old heart could take another rescue mission."

Lily laughed, a slight blush coloring her cheeks. "Don't worry, that lesson was definitely learned. No more sneaking off to mysterious islands for me."

"Besides," Aaron added, wrapping an arm around his daughter's shoulders, "I'll be keeping a much closer eye on her this time. Can't be too careful in this town, from what we've read in the papers."

I raised an eyebrow. "Oh? And what exactly have you been reading?"

"Everything!" Lily exclaimed. "We've been following all your cases. The Valentine's Day poisoning, the dead champion in the bar... though I have to say, some of the details seemed a bit... exaggerated? I'd love to hear how things really went down."

I sniffed my armpit and winced. The run had left me smelling like a particularly pungent locker room. "Tell you what," I said, "why don't we meet up in a bit? Say, around ten? I'll shower, and then we can head to the Easter Fair together. I'll fill you in on all the less sensational details on the way."

After agreeing on a meeting time, we said our goodbyes. As Ginger and I headed back to the house, I could feel my legs turning to jelly with each step. The sidewalk seemed to stretch endlessly before me, and I briefly considered the merits of simply lying down right there and becoming one with the concrete.

The moment we were through the front door, I collapsed onto the living room couch with a groan that seemed to come from the depths of my aching muscles. The old springs creaked in protest, as if sharing my pain.

"Finally," I mumbled into a throw pillow. "I thought I was going to pass out right there on the sidewalk."

Ginger leapt onto the coffee table, his tail swishing with amusement. "Oh no, you don't. We've got a schedule to keep, old man. Shower, breakfast, and then off to the Fair. No time for dramatic fainting."

I waved a hand weakly in his direction. "Just five minutes. That's all I need. A quick power nap to rejuvenate the old bones."

"Jim," Ginger's voice took on a warning tone. "Don't make me wake you up the hard way. Remember what happened last time?"

Images of ice-cold water and strategically placed claws flashed through my mind. With a herculean effort, I pushed myself up off the couch. "Alright, alright. I'm moving. But I want it noted that this is cruel and unusual punishment."

"Duly noted," Ginger replied cheerfully. "Now march, Detective Butterfield. That shower won't take itself. And may I suggest using extra soap? You're a bit ripe, even by human standards."

***

An hour later, freshly showered and feeling marginally more human, I found myself walking toward the town square with Aaron, Lily, and Ginger. The morning air was warm and pleasant, carrying the promise of a beautiful spring day. The scent of blooming flowers mingled with the salty tang of the nearby ocean, creating a uniquely Oceanview Cove perfume.

As we walked, I regaled them with the true stories behind our recent cases, carefully editing out some of the more harrowing details. Lily hung on every word, her eyes wide with excitement as I described our adventures.

"So let me get this straight," Lily said, her eyes wide with excitement. "You actually caught the killer using toy mice?"

I nodded, unable to suppress a grin. "It was Ginger's finest hour. You should have seen him, chasing those mechanical rodents around like his life depended on it."

Ginger, trotting along beside us, let out an indignant meow. "I'll have you know that was a masterful performance. My reputation in the feline community may never recover."

We rounded the corner, and the town square came into view. I blinked, momentarily taken aback by the transformation. Just hours ago, the square had been a flurry of last-minute preparations. Now, it was a vibrant spectacle of color and activity. Fully set up tents and booths dotted the area, their bright banners flapping in the gentle breeze. Excited chatter filled the air as visitors bustled through the square, taking in the festive atmosphere.

The air was filled with a cacophony of sounds – children laughing, vendors calling out their wares. The smell of cotton candy and fresh popcorn wafted through the air, making my stomach growl despite our recent breakfast.

"Wow," Lily breathed, her eyes darting from one attraction to another. "This is amazing! We don't have anything like this back home."

Aaron nodded in agreement. "It's certainly... festive. Looks like the whole town has turned out for this."

As we approached the entrance to the Fair, my eyes were drawn to a familiar figure manning the first tent. Mrs. Henderson, resplendent in a hat that seemed to be trying to encompass the entire Easter theme in one improbable structure, waved enthusiastically as we approached.

"I see you survived your morning run, Mr. Butterfield!" she called out, her voice carrying over the din of the Fair. "And who are these lovely guests?"

I introduced Aaron and Lily, explaining that Lily was the girl who had gone missing last year.

Mrs. Henderson's eyes lit up with recognition. "Oh my, of course! There was so much gossip when you went missing, dear. Such a relief when you were found safe and sound."

As we drew closer to the tent, I realized why Mrs. Henderson had abandoned her usual post on her porch. The tent was filled to bursting with books – dozens, perhaps hundreds of identical volumes stacked neatly on tables and shelves.

"Mrs. Henderson," I said, unable to keep the surprise from my voice, "what's all this? Don't tell me you've become an author in your spare time?"

She beamed at me, her eyes twinkling with mischief. "Indeed I have, Mr. Butterfield! Allow me to present my magnum opus – 'Whispers on the Wind: Twenty Years of East Coast Gossip and Mysteries'!"

She thrust a book into my hands. The cover featured a slightly airbrushed photo of Mrs. Henderson herself, peering dramatically over a pair of binoculars. In the background, I could make out what looked like a collection of minivans in varying states of suspiciousness. I blinked, momentarily at a loss for words.

"This is... impressive," I managed finally. "But how on earth did you manage to get this published? I didn't think 'Professional Gossip' was a recognized literary genre."

Mrs. Henderson waved a hand dismissively, nearly dislodging a small stuffed chick from her hat in the process. "Oh, it was nothing, really. My son-in-law works for some fancy publishing house up in New York. He tried to turn me down at first, can you believe it? Said something about 'liability concerns' and 'fact-checking.' Nonsense! But my daughter Evelyn, bless her heart, has a way of being very... persuasive."

Aaron leaned in, his curiosity piqued. "And what exactly is this book about, Mrs. Henderson?"

She drew herself up, puffing out her chest with pride. "It's a comprehensive collection of all the gossip, rumors, and unsolved mysteries I've documented over the past two decades! Eyewitness accounts, suspicious happenings, even reports from Barbara's cousin up in Maine. It's all here, every juicy detail!"

"I bet it is," Ginger muttered. "The definitive guide to minivan-based conspiracies and seagull espionage, no doubt. I can't wait for the movie adaptation. Maybe they'll get Daniel Craig to play the lead minivan."

I stifled a laugh, covering it with a cough. "That sounds... thorough, Mrs. Henderson. Maybe next time I'll-"

"I'll take one!" Lily interrupted, her eyes shining with excitement.

Aaron started to protest. "Now, Lily, I'm not sure if-"

But Mrs. Henderson was already wrapping up a copy, her hands moving with surprising speed for someone her age. The book disappeared into a bag adorned with cartoon minivans before Aaron could finish his sentence.

"That's the spirit, dear!" she crowed. "You know, there's a whole chapter dedicated to your adventure on that island. Oh, and of course, all of Mr. Butterfield and Ginger's cases are in here too. My own personal theories included."

Aaron sighed, reaching for his wallet. "Well, I suppose it could be... educational."

As we walked away from Mrs. Henderson's tent, I couldn't help but wonder what outlandish versions of our cases we'd find within its pages. Something told me that Mrs. Henderson's "personal theories" would be more creative than factual.

We continued through the Fair, taking in the sights and sounds. Vendors hawked everything from hand-knitted Easter bunnies to artisanal cheeses shaped like eggs.

As we rounded a corner, I spotted a familiar face behind one of the booths. Shawn, looking slightly harried but still managing his usual charming grin, was surrounded by a crowd of excited children. He appeared to be selling... cocktails?

"Hold on a second," I said to Aaron and Lily. "I want to introduce you to a friend of mine. Though I'm a bit concerned about what exactly he's serving to those kids."

We approached Shawn's booth, weaving through the throng of excited children. As we got closer, I could see that the drinks Shawn was mixing were colorful concoctions topped with whipped cream and sprinkles.

"Shawn," I called out, raising an eyebrow. "Please tell me there's no alcohol in those."

Shawn looked up, his face breaking into a wide grin. "Jim! Of course not, what do you take me for? I'm mastering the art of kid-friendly cocktails by day, adult beverages by night. I'm practically Batman."

A small boy in a Batman t-shirt, who had been eagerly slurping a bright blue drink, perked up at this. "Batman? He's the best superhero ever!"

This declaration was immediately met with protest from another boy, this one sporting a Superman baseball cap. "No way! Superman is way cooler than Batman!"

The two boys began to argue, their voices rising above the general din of the Fair. Their mother, looking slightly frazzled, quickly ushered them away, mouthing an apology to Shawn as she went.

Shawn chuckled, shaking his head. "Never a dull moment. Now, who do we have here? I don't believe we've met."

I gestured to Aaron and Lily. "Shawn, I'd like you to meet Aaron and his daughter Lily. Remember that case with the missing girl on the island? This is her."

Recognition dawned on Shawn's face. "Of course! I remember now. It's a shame you didn't get a chance to visit the Salty Breeze last time you were in town."

Aaron smiled. "Well, we've got a bit more time on our hands this visit. We'll definitely stop by."

"You should," I added. "Shawn here actually helped us find Lily, in a way. He realized where the lighthouse beam was approximately pointing in that painting, which led us to the tunnels and eventually the island."

Lily's eyes widened. "Really? Thank you so much! I can't believe how many people were involved in finding me. I feel like I should be handing out thank-you cards or something."

Shawn waved off her thanks with a modest smile. "It was nothing, really. Any halfway decent bartender could have done the same. Now, what can I get you folks? And remember, it's strictly non-alcoholic today."

We placed our orders, and Shawn set to work, his hands moving with practiced ease as he mixed and garnished our drinks. As he worked, he chatted easily with Aaron and Lily, asking about their visit and sharing some of the funnier stories from the Salty Breeze.

Drinks in hand, we bid Shawn farewell, promising to stop by the bar later that evening. As we moved away from his booth, I took a sip of my drink and was pleasantly surprised. Even without alcohol, Shawn's mixology skills were impressive.

We continued our tour of the Fair, stopping occasionally to admire local crafts or sample treats from the food vendors. The square was getting more crowded as the morning wore on, filled with families enjoying the festivities.

I spotted another familiar face. Emma's tent stood out among the others, now fully set up and looking much more impressive than it had during our early morning run. It was draped in shimmering fabrics and adorned with twinkling lights. A long line of people waited outside, all eager for a glimpse into their futures.

"Looks like Emma wasn't exaggerating about this being her busiest day of the year," I remarked. "Want to see what all the fuss is about? I promise, her predictions are at least 60% less ominous than they sound."

Aaron and Lily nodded eagerly, and we joined the queue. As we waited, I could hear snatches of conversation from those leaving Emma's tent – excited whispers about love, success, and mysterious strangers. One woman clutched a crystal to her chest, muttering something about "aligning her chakras with the cosmic Easter bunny." I decided not to ask.

When it was finally our turn, Emma's face lit up with recognition. "Aaron!" she exclaimed. "The stars told me you would return to our little town, but I didn't expect it to be so soon!"

Aaron chuckled, shaking his head in amusement. "I'm still impressed by how you handled Sheriff Miller when we were looking for Lily. Speaking of which," he gently nudged Lily forward, "I don't believe you two have officially met."

Emma's gaze fell on Lily, and her eyes widened. "Ah, of course! I can feel the connection between you two. The stars never lie, you know."

Lily looked at Emma with a mixture of curiosity and skepticism. "Can you really sense that?"

"Of course, dear," Emma replied, her voice taking on a mystical quality. "The universe speaks to those who know how to listen. And right now, it's telling me that you're due for a free reading. What do you say?"

Lily glanced at her father, who nodded encouragingly. "Um, sure," she said, a hint of excitement creeping into her voice. "Why not?"

Emma beamed, ushering Lily to a small table covered in a deep purple cloth. She pulled out a variety of tools – crystals, tarot cards, and a crystal ball that caught the light in mesmerizing ways.

"Now, my dear," Emma said, her voice low and mysterious, "let's see what the universe has in store for you."

What followed was a performance worthy of a stage magician. Emma waved her hands over the crystal ball, muttering incantations under her breath. She arranged and rearranged her crystals in patterns that seemed to have some significance, at least to her. Tarot cards were drawn, examined with great seriousness, and laid out in an intricate spread.

Throughout it all, Lily watched with wide-eyed fascination, while Aaron tried (and failed) to hide his amused skepticism. Ginger, curled up at my feet, let out a soft snort.

"I see Emma's flair for the dramatic hasn't diminished," he muttered. "Though I have to admit, her crystal juggling skills are impressive."

Finally, after what seemed like an eternity of mystical gestures and cryptic muttering, Emma sat back with a satisfied sigh. "Ah, yes," she said, her voice filled with portent. "The stars have spoken, my dear Lily."

Lily leaned forward eagerly, nearly knocking over a precariously balanced tower of crystals. "What did they say?"

Emma's expression turned serious, her brow furrowing as if she was deciphering a particularly tricky bit of cosmic code. "You will witness misfortune, Lily. But don't worry! The stars say you'll play an important part in making things right. The path might not be clear at first, but trust yourself and those around you. Great things are coming your way!"

As Emma's words hung in the air, I felt a sudden chill run down my spine. It was probably just the breeze, I told myself. After all, Emma's predictions were usually vague enough to fit any situation. And yet...

I couldn't shake the feeling that her words held more weight than usual. Whatever was coming, I had a feeling our Easter weekend was about to become a lot more interesting than we'd bargained for.

Chapter 3

As we moved away from Emma's tent, the vibrant sounds and smells of the Easter Fair enveloped us once again. Children laughed and squealed as they played carnival games, the cheerful music provided a festive backdrop.

"So," Aaron said, his eyebrows raised skeptically, "how accurate are Emma's predictions usually? That was quite a dramatic reading she gave Lily."

I chuckled, remembering some of Emma's more colorful prophecies from recent months. "It's hard to say, really. Emma certainly has a flair for the dramatic. But I have to admit, sometimes her predictions are eerily on point."

"Like what?" Lily asked eagerly, her eyes shining with curiosity.

"Well," I said, "when I first moved to Oceanview Cove, Emma warned me that trouble was brewing. She said the stars foretold 'dark clouds on my horizon' or something equally ominous. I brushed it off at the time, but wouldn't you know it, the very next day I found myself a suspect in a murder investigation."

Aaron's eyebrows shot up. "Wait a minute, I remember Emma mentioning something about that on the way to the police station when we were looking for Lily."

Lily's eyes widened. "Seriously? You were a murder suspect?"

I nodded, remembering those tense early days in town. "It's a long story, but yes. Thankfully Ginger and I managed to solve the case and clear my name. But ever since then, I've learned not to completely discount Emma's predictions. Sometimes they're so accurate it's a bit terrifying."

Lily's face lit up with excitement. "In that case, I hope this prediction comes true! I'd love to play a crucial role in something important. Maybe there's a reason Dad and I are visiting Oceanview Cove again."

I glanced at her, struck by the earnestness in her voice. "You know, Lily, you might not be far off. I can't explain it, but I've had this feeling all day that something is coming. Like the calm before a storm."

"Jim, your talent for ominous foreshadowing is rivaled only by your ability to attract trouble," Ginger muttered. "Though I suppose in this town, trouble finds us whether we're looking for it or not."

As if on cue, we approached the center of the town square where a large crowd had gathered. Children of all ages jostled for position, their faces alight with anticipation. Among them, I spotted Leo bouncing on his toes next to Olivia, who gave me a friendly wave.

At the front of the crowd stood Mayor Thompson, his round face flushed with excitement (and quite possibly the effects of sampling too many pastries). He held a megaphone in one hand and was gesturing expansively with the other.

"Ladies and gentlemen, boys and girls!" the Mayor's voice boomed through the megaphone. "It's time for the main event you've all been waiting for – the Great Oceanview Cove Easter Egg Hunt!"

A cheer went up from the assembled children. Mayor Thompson beamed, clearly in his element. "Now, this isn't just any old egg hunt. Oh no! You'll be searching for one very special egg hidden somewhere here in the square. It could be in one of the tents, behind a booth, or cleverly camouflaged anywhere else. Observe!"

He held up a large plastic egg, painted in swirls of pastel colors with intricate designs. "This is what you're looking for, kids! Well, not this exact egg – that would be too easy. But one that looks just like it!"

As the Mayor continued explaining the rules, his gaze swept over the crowd and landed on me. A grin spread across his face that made me instantly wary.

"Jim, Ginger, why don't you join in?" he asked. "Show these youngsters how it's done – give them a real detective master class!"

I felt my face grow hot as every eye in the crowd turned toward me. "Oh, that's very kind, Mayor, but I wouldn't want to ruin the children's fun. This is their game, after all."

A chorus of protests erupted from the kids. "No way!"

"We'll find it first!"

"Yeah, we can beat a grown-up!"

Aaron chuckled beside me, clearly amused by my discomfort. "Come on, Jim. You can't disappoint your adoring public. Where's your sense of adventure?"

I shot him a look that I hoped conveyed my deep reluctance. But seeing the eager faces of the children, I knew I was fighting a losing battle.

With a deep sigh of resignation, I turned to Lily. "What about you? You're technically still a kid too. Want to join in and save me from complete humiliation?"

Lily grinned and shook her head. "No way. I'd much rather watch from the sidelines and pick up some professional detective techniques. You know, for future reference."

"Traitor," I muttered, but there was no real heat in it.

Squaring my shoulders, I addressed the Mayor. "Alright, you win. Ginger and I will participate. All in the name of passing on valuable detective experience to the next generation."

"Excellent!" Mayor Thompson boomed. "You heard it, folks! Man versus child in the ultimate egg-hunting showdown! Who will emerge victorious?"

As the Mayor began the official countdown, I glanced down at Ginger. To my surprise, his eyes were narrowed in concentration, his tail twitching with what I recognized as pre-pounce excitement.

"Planning your strategy?" I murmured.

Ginger's whiskers quivered. "Oh, I'm going to show these amateurs how it's done. Prepare yourself, Jim. You're about to witness the ultimate display of feline superiority."

Before I could respond, Mayor Thompson's voice rang out: "On your marks... get set... GO!"

What followed was nothing short of chaos. Children scattered in every direction, their excited shrieks filling the air as they upended flower pots, peered under benches, and swarmed through tents. I found myself swept along in their wake, trying (and largely failing) to maintain some semblance of dignity as I joined the search.

"This is ridiculous," I muttered to myself as I halfheartedly peered behind a trash can. "I'm a grown man playing hide-and-seek with children."

"Less complaining, more searching," Ginger meowed from somewhere near my feet. "Your lack of enthusiasm is embarrassing. Watch and learn."

With that, he darted off, weaving between legs and leaping onto tables with feline agility. I couldn't help but admire his determination, even if I thought this whole endeavor was slightly absurd.

As the hunt continued, I witnessed scenes that would have been comical if I wasn't right in the middle of them. Two young boys got into a tug-of-war over a regular chicken egg someone had apparently dropped, each insisting it was the special egg in disguise. A little girl in a frilly dress climbed halfway up a tree before her mother, red-faced and apologetic, had to coax her back down. Emma, caught up in the excitement, was attempting to divine the egg's location by tossing crystals onto the ground, much to the bewilderment of passing children.

And through it all, I bumbled along, feeling more and more like a bull in a china shop with each passing minute. Every time I thought I spotted something egg-shaped, a small body would invariably dart in front of me, snatching it up with a triumphant cry only to toss it aside in disappointment moments later.

After what felt like hours but was probably only about twenty minutes, I found myself near the entrance of the square. My hair was disheveled, my clothes were rumpled, and I was pretty sure I had somehow acquired a smear of face paint on my cheek. I was seriously considering admitting defeat when something caught my eye.

There, perched atop Mrs. Henderson's elaborate hat like the world's most obvious hiding place, sat the special egg.

I blinked, sure I must be seeing things. But no – there it was, nestled among the riot of spring flowers and miniature rabbits that adorned her headwear. How on earth had I missed that earlier? More importantly, how had Mrs. Henderson herself not noticed?

As I stood there, momentarily dumbstruck, I felt a tug on my sleeve. I looked down to see Leo, his face etched with worry.

"Uncle Jim," he whispered, "I can't find the egg anywhere. What if I'm not a good detective after all?"

My heart melted at the disappointment in his voice. Making a split-second decision, I crouched down to his level.

"Hey now, don't give up," I said softly. "A good detective never stops looking. In fact..." I leaned in closer, lowering my voice conspiratorially. "I think I might have spotted something. But you have to promise not to tell anyone I helped you, okay?"

Leo's eyes widened, and he nodded solemnly.

I discreetly pointed toward Mrs. Henderson. "Take a close look at Mrs. Henderson's hat."

Leo's face lit up with understanding. He gave me a quick nod before scampering off toward Mrs. Henderson.

"Mrs. Henderson!" he called out. "I found it! The special egg is on your hat!"

A hush fell over the square, followed quickly by a surge of excitement as everyone realized Leo was right. Mrs. Henderson herself looked comically startled, her hands flying to her head as if to confirm that yes, there really was an egg perched up there.

"Well, I'll be!" she exclaimed. "How in the world did that get there? I didn't feel a thing!"

Mayor Thompson's voice boomed out once again. "Ladies and gentlemen, we have a winner! Young Leo Reeves has found the special egg! And in record time too – even faster than our professional detectives!"

As Leo was presented with his prize – a large Easter basket overflowing with candy and small toys – I caught Ginger's eye. He was primly grooming himself, the very picture of feline nonchalance.

"Not a word," he muttered.

I couldn't quite hold back my smirk. "Wouldn't dream of it, partner. Though I have to say, for someone who was going to show these amateurs how it's done..."

Ginger's tail lashed once, cutting me off. "Yes, well. Clearly, the egg's location was too obvious. Any self-respecting feline would have dismissed it immediately as too easy. It's not my fault humans lack our sophisticated reasoning skills."

I wisely chose not to point out that I had, in fact, spotted the egg. Some arguments just weren't worth having.

As the excitement began to die down, Mayor Thompson addressed the crowd once more.

"What a thrilling hunt that was! Now, I see we have quite a few visitors with us today." He beamed at the assembled tourists. "Before you leave, make sure to stop by our town museum and see the real gem of Oceanview Cove – our very own precious Easter Egg! It was discovered by archaeologists right here near our town several years ago. A true historical treasure!"

Lily tugged on my sleeve, her eyes shining with curiosity. "A precious Easter Egg? What's that all about?"

I wracked my brain, trying to remember the details. "You know, I think Shawn mentioned something about it a while back. To be honest, I've never actually seen it myself. Always meant to, but you know how it is – too busy solving murders to be a proper tourist in my own town."

"Well, why don't we go check it out now?" Aaron suggested. "Before all these kids and their candy-fueled excitement descend on the place."

It seemed like a good idea to me. Plus, I was more than ready to escape the lingering embarrassment of the egg hunt. "Sounds great. Let's head over there now."

As we made our way toward the exit of the square, I noticed another familiar face staffing a booth near the edge of the Fair. Mrs. Abernathy stood behind a table laden with an impressive array of cookies, Mr. Whiskers perched regally beside her like some sort of feline quality control supervisor.

"I see His Royal Feline Majesty is maintaining his lofty standards of cookie supervision," Ginger muttered, eyeing Mr. Whiskers. The other cat merely blinked lazily in response, the picture of nonchalance.

As we approached, I noticed Mrs. Abernathy handing out cookies to passersby.

"Mrs. Abernathy!" I called out in greeting. "Back to handing out your delicious treats, I see."

She smiled warmly at us. "Of course, dear. That time at the boat racing tournament was a one-off thing."

I introduced Lily and Aaron, explaining that they were visiting for the Fair. As I mentioned we were headed to the museum to see the famous Easter Egg, Mrs. Abernathy's eyes lit up.

"Oh, you must try some of these cookies for the road then," she insisted, already packing up a small bag. "Can't have you touring on an empty stomach."

As she handed over the treats, I asked, "By the way, where are Sophie and Alice? I saw them preparing some goodies this morning."

Mrs. Abernathy nodded. "They'll be taking over in the afternoon. Though I doubt they'll be as generous with the freebies as I am. Got to make a profit sometime, after all!"

We thanked her for the cookies and continued on our way, munching contentedly as we walked. Lily and Aaron's eyes widened at the first bite.

"These are incredible!" Lily exclaimed. "I've never tasted cookies like this before."

Aaron nodded in agreement. "Seriously, Jim. The baked goods alone might be worth the trip back to Oceanview Cove."

I grinned, feeling a surge of pride in my adopted hometown. "They are pretty spectacular, aren't they? Though I will say, you have to be a bit careful around here. Sometimes the pastries can be a little too exciting, if you know what I mean."

Lily's eyes widened. "Are you hinting at the Valentine's Day poisoning case?"

I nodded, impressed by her quick deduction. "Exactly. But don't worry – Mrs. Abernathy's treats are guaranteed to be poison-free!"

Despite my reassurance, I noticed Aaron eyeing his half-eaten cookie with slightly more caution than before.

***

As we approached the museum, I felt a familiar sense of anticipation building. It was the same feeling I got at the start of a new case – a mixture of excitement and trepidation, knowing that something interesting was just around the corner.

The Oceanview Cove Historical Museum was housed in a stately Victorian mansion, its white paint gleaming in the late morning sun. As we climbed the steps to the entrance, I couldn't help but admire the intricate gingerbread trim and the way the sunlight caught the stained-glass windows.

The heavy wooden door creaked open, revealing a dim, cool interior that smelled faintly of old books and furniture polish. As our eyes adjusted to the lower light, a familiar figure approached us from behind the reception desk.

"Welcome to the Oceanview Cove Historical Museum," she said warmly, then paused as recognition dawned.

"Well, if it isn't Mr. Butterfield and Ginger! And... Lily? My goodness, how you've grown!"

I smiled, pleased to see a friendly face. "Hello, Dorothy. It's good to see you again. You remember Lily, of course. And this is her father, Aaron."

Dorothy beamed at us all. "Of course I remember! I was so relieved when I heard you'd been found safe and sound, dear. And it's a pleasure to meet you, Aaron. I can certainly see the family resemblance."

As Dorothy and Aaron exchanged pleasantries, I found myself remembering the last time Ginger and I had been here. It felt like a lifetime ago, poring over that painting of the shipwreck, trying to piece together clues to find Lily.

"So," Dorothy said, clapping her hands together. "What brings you all to our humble museum today? Not another mystery to solve, I hope?"

I chuckled. "No, nothing like that. We're actually here to see the famous Easter Egg everyone's been talking about. Thought we'd check it out before the crowds from the Fair descend."

Dorothy's face lit up. "Ah, yes! Our pride and joy. Well, you're in for a treat. Follow me, and I'll tell you all about it on the way."

As we made our way through the museum's winding corridors, Dorothy regaled us with the history of the egg. Apparently, it had been discovered during an archaeological dig just outside of town about a decade ago. The Fabergé egg, which dated back to the early 18th century, was made of solid gold and encrusted with precious gems. It was dubbed the "Easter Egg" due to its discovery on Easter Sunday.

"The craftsmanship is simply exquisite," Dorothy enthused as we walked. "Each jewel was hand-set with incredible precision. And the engravings! They tell a fascinating story of the town's early days. It's truly a remarkable piece of our history."

As we approached the room where the egg was displayed, I noticed a sign blocking the entrance. "Cleaning in Progress," it read in bold red letters.

Dorothy frowned, her brow furrowing in confusion. "That's odd."

Just then, a young man wearing glasses and a janitor's uniform emerged from a nearby room, pushing a cart laden with cleaning supplies. His long, greasy hair was tied back in a messy ponytail.

"Ah, Josh," Dorothy called out. "Did you finish cleaning the Easter Egg Room? We have some guests who'd like to see it."

Josh looked puzzled, adjusting his glasses as he glanced at the sign. "That's weird, Ms. Collins. I cleaned the Easter Egg Room first thing this morning, just like you asked. I'm not sure who moved the sign from the Modern History Room I was cleaning in."

A flicker of worry crossed Dorothy's face. She hurried forward, removing the sign and pushing open the door.

We followed close behind, a sense of unease growing in the pit of my stomach.

The room was dimly lit, shadows pooling in the corners. In the center stood a glass display case, illuminated by a soft spotlight from above. But as we drew closer, my heart sank.

The case was empty.

Chapter 4

The silence in the room was deafening as we all stared at the empty display case. Dorothy's face had gone pale, her eyes wide with disbelief. She stepped forward, her hand hovering over the glass as if she couldn't quite believe what she was seeing. The soft hum of the museum's air conditioning seemed unnaturally loud in the stunned quiet.

"This... this can't be," she whispered, her voice trembling. "The egg was here just this morning. I checked it myself before opening."

I moved closer to examine the case, my detective instincts kicking in despite the shock. The smell of glass cleaner and polished wood filled my nostrils as I leaned in. That's when I noticed something odd about the glass. There was a perfect circle cut out at the top, barely visible unless you were looking for it.

"Dorothy," I said, pointing to the cut. "Look at this."

She leaned in, squinting through her glasses. When she saw the circular cut, she gasped, her breath fogging the glass slightly. "How is that possible? We installed specially reinforced glass to protect the egg. It would take industrial-grade tools to cut through it so cleanly."

As Dorothy spoke, a nagging feeling tugged at the back of my mind. I'd seen something like this before, but I couldn't quite place where. The memory danced just out of reach, frustratingly elusive, like trying to remember a dream upon waking.

"We have to call the police right away," Dorothy declared, her voice rising with panic. Her hands fluttered nervously, straightening her already impeccable cardigan.

I exchanged a glance with Aaron, both of us no doubt remembering the less-than-stellar performance of Oceanview Cove's law enforcement during Lily's disappearance. His raised eyebrow spoke volumes.

"You're right," I agreed, trying to keep my voice calm and reassuring. "The police might not be much help, but at least they can seal off the museum as a crime scene. Though I hate to think how the townsfolk will react, especially on Easter when everyone wants to see the egg."

"Well, there's nothing to see now, is there?" Ginger muttered, his tail swishing with agitation. "Unless they'd like to admire an empty glass case."

I turned to Dorothy and said, "Call the police and close the museum completely. No one leaves until they arrive."

Dorothy nodded, already pulling out her cell phone. Her fingers trembled slightly as she dialed. "I'll do that right away and head to the security room. We need to lock this place down."

As she hurried toward the exit, her heels clicking rapidly on the polished floor, Josh, the janitor, stepped forward. He fidgeted with the mop in his hands, looking uncertain. "I should help her close all the exits," he offered, moving to follow Dorothy.

"Actually, Josh," I said, my voice firm but not unkind, "I think it would be best if you stayed here. We have some questions for you."

Josh's face fell, a flicker of unease crossing his features. But he nodded and remained where he was, fidgeting with the hem of his uniform shirt. The strong smell of cleaning products wafted from his clothes as he shifted nervously.

Lily, who had been examining the empty display case with the intensity of a seasoned detective, suddenly perked up. Her eyes sparkled with excitement as she turned to us. "You know," she said, her voice pitched higher with enthusiasm, "this must be the misfortune Emma was talking about in her prediction. The one I was supposed to witness!"

I couldn't help but smile at her enthusiasm. "You're right, Lily. We'll have to add this to Emma's list of correct predictions."

"Don't forget the second part of the prediction," Aaron chimed in. "Emma said Lily would be part of fixing it too. Looks like you'll be helping us find the egg, kiddo."

Lily's face lit up at the prospect, her smile wide enough to rival the Easter Bunny's. "Really? I can help investigate?" She bounced on her toes, practically vibrating with excitement.

"Absolutely," I said, warming to the idea. "In fact, why don't you and your dad start by examining the room? Look for anything that seems out of place or unusual." I added quietly, "Ginger, why don't you join them?"

"Wonderful," Ginger muttered, his whiskers twitching with dry amusement. "I'll be sure to use my keen feline senses to sniff out any egg-shaped clues."

As Lily and Aaron began their search, with Ginger padding along behind them, I turned my attention back to Josh. The janitor was a mess of nervous energy, his eyes darting around the room as if searching for an escape route. A bead of sweat trickled down his temple despite the cool air in the museum.

Before I could begin questioning him, Josh blurted out, "It's all my fault! The egg being stolen, I mean. The police are going to suspect me first, aren't they? Oh god, I'm going to jail. I can't go to jail! Do you know what they do to janitors in prison?"

I held up a hand, trying to calm him down. "Slow down, Josh. No one's suspecting you of anything yet. And I'm pretty sure there's no special prison treatment for janitors. We just need to clarify a few things and establish a timeline of events. Why don't we start from the beginning? Walk me through your day, from the moment you arrived at work this morning."

Josh took a deep breath, visibly trying to compose himself. He ran a hand through his greasy ponytail, inadvertently leaving a streak of dust in his hair. "Right, okay. Well, I got here early today, around 7 AM. I wanted to make sure all the exhibit rooms were ready for visitors, especially the Easter Egg Room. So I started there, like Ms. Collins asked, gave it a thorough cleaning. Dusted the display case, mopped the floors, even got rid of a cobweb in the corner that's been taunting me for days."

"Alright," I said. "Did you notice anything strange today? Any visitors who seemed overly interested in the egg, or just suspicious in general? Maybe someone lurking around with a giant Easter basket and a mischievous glint in their eye?"

Josh shook his head emphatically, his ponytail whipping back and forth. "It was dead quiet all morning. No visitors at all. Everyone was at the Easter Fair in the square. I didn't even have to ask anyone to leave while I was cleaning. Though," he added, his brow furrowing, "I did see a squirrel outside the window that looked pretty shifty. Do you think squirrels can steal Easter eggs?"

I bit back a sigh. "I think we can rule out squirrels as suspects for now, Josh. Let's go back a bit. You said earlier that you thought the egg being stolen was your fault. Why is that?"

Josh's face fell, and he slumped against his mop like it was the only thing holding him up. "Well, after finishing the Easter Egg exhibit first thing this morning, I moved on to other areas. I was working in the Modern History Room – you know, where I came out of earlier? When I entered, I put up the 'Cleaning in Progress' sign. The cleaning took longer than usual because I accidentally spilled my coffee. I was juggling my mop and coffee while reaching for my phone – thought I heard a TikTok notification – and then bam! Coffee everywhere. While I was cleaning up that mess, someone must have moved the sign to the Easter Egg Room and stolen the egg. If I hadn't been so clumsy, maybe I would have caught them!"

A thought struck me. "Wait a second, shouldn't there be security cameras in this room?"

Before Josh could answer, Lily's voice rang out from across the room. "Mr. Butterfield! I think I found something weird on the camera!"

I hurried over to where Lily was standing, pointing up at a security camera mounted in the corner of the room. As I got closer, I could see what had caught her attention – there was a piece of paper fully covering the camera lens.

"Good eye, Lily," I said, impressed. "We need to get that paper down and see what it is."

Josh, eager to be helpful, piped up. "I have a ladder I use for cleaning high places. The spider webs up there accumulate really fast. I swear, sometimes I think the spiders are having parties in the corners. I can go get it."

I nodded. "That would be great, Josh. Thank you."

As Josh hurried off to fetch the ladder, I turned back to Lily. "Nice work, detective," I said with a smile. "You've got sharp eyes. Keep this up, and you'll be solving cases on your own in no time."

Lily beamed at the praise, practically glowing with pride. "Thanks! I can't wait to see what that paper is. Maybe it's a ransom note from the egg thief! Or a map to their secret hideout!"

I chuckled at her enthusiasm. "Let's not get ahead of ourselves. For all we know, it could just be a takeout menu that got very, very lost."

Josh returned quickly with the ladder, setting it up beneath the camera. The old wooden ladder groaned as he positioned it, making me wonder if it was older than some of the museum exhibits. He started to climb, but Lily stopped him.

"Wait," she said, her eyes shining with excitement. "I found it, so... can I get it down? Please? I promise I'll be careful!"

I hesitated for a moment, then nodded. "Alright, but be careful. And here," I said, handing her one of my latex gloves. "Put this on first. We don't want to contaminate any potential evidence."

Lily pulled on the glove, and then climbed the ladder with surprising agility. She carefully peeled the paper off the camera lens and climbed back down, holding it out for us to see with the reverence of someone handling a priceless artifact.

"It looks like... a photograph?" she said, peering at it closely.

I took the paper, examining it carefully. "You're right. It's a photo of this room, taken from the camera's point of view. Look, you can see the display case with the egg still in it. Our thief is cleverer than we thought."

Aaron whistled low. "Clever. They put this up to fool the security cameras, make it look like nothing was happening in here. I've got to admit, that's pretty ingenious."

"I've seen stuff like this in spy movies," Lily added excitedly. "But I never thought it would actually work in real life! Do you think the thief was wearing all black and humming the Mission Impossible theme while they did it?"

Just then, Dorothy burst back into the room, looking flustered. Her usually impeccable hair was slightly disheveled, and she was slightly out of breath. "I've called the police," she announced. "All the exits are locked, and I've got our security guard watching the camera feed. He says he didn't see anything unusual, though."

I held up the photograph we'd found. "That's because of this. The thief covered the camera with a photo of the room, making it look like nothing had changed. It's like a magician's trick, but with more felony charges."

Dorothy's face paled as she took in this new information. "But... but what about Ben? He was supposed to be patrolling the rooms! Don't tell me he was fooled by a photograph too?"

"Ben?" I asked, raising an eyebrow.

"Our other security guard," Dorothy explained, looking increasingly frazzled. "But he's nowhere to be found. I can't reach him on his radio. It's like he's vanished into thin air! First the egg, now Ben... what's next? Will we discover the dinosaur bones have decided to take a stroll?"

Josh cleared his throat nervously, shifting from foot to foot. "I, uh, I think I might know where Ben is," he said, looking like he'd rather be anywhere else. "When I was cleaning the bathrooms about an hour ago, he came rushing in looking pretty green."

Dorothy sighed, pinching the bridge of her nose. "Wonderful. So one guard is indisposed, and the other was fooled by a photograph. How are we supposed to find the egg and the thief now?"

As if in answer to Dorothy's question, Ginger let out a sharp meow from the far corner of the room. I hurried over to see what had caught his attention, grateful for the distraction from the increasingly absurd situation.

"What is it, Ginger?" I asked quietly. "Please tell me you haven't found a nest of security-guard-eating spiders."

Ginger nodded toward the wall. "That vent looks a bit off, don't you think? Like someone's been messing with it. Unless the museum has very ambitious mice with a penchant for modern art."

I followed his gaze and noticed he was right. The vent cover was slightly askew, as if it had been recently removed and hastily replaced. It was a small detail, easy to miss if you weren't looking for it, but it stood out like a sore thumb now that Ginger had pointed it out.

"Good catch," I murmured to Ginger, then turned to the others. "Josh, could you bring the ladder over here? I think we've found something."

As Josh maneuvered the ladder into place, Lily started forward eagerly. "I can climb up again-"

I shook my head, cutting her off gently. "Not this time, Lily. We don't know what might be in there. It could be dangerous, or worse, really dusty. I'll check it out."

"Oh, sure," Ginger muttered. "Send the old man with questionable upper body strength up the rickety ladder. What could possibly go wrong? I'll just be down here, ready to call the paramedics when you inevitably fall and discover new and exciting ways to embarrass yourself."

Ignoring Ginger's less-than-encouraging commentary, I made my way up the ladder. It creaked ominously under my weight, and I found myself wishing I'd taken Ginger's exercise regimen more seriously. Or at least that I'd eaten one less toast this morning.

Reaching the vent, I slipped on my remaining glove before removing the cover. Even through the latex, the metal felt cool to the touch. A faint draft wafted from the opening as I peered inside, half-expecting to see a tiny sign saying "Egg Thief Was Here." Instead, I spotted something that didn't belong – a small, metallic object wedged just inside the vent.

I gently extracted the item. It was heavier than expected, with a sleek, professional design that spoke of high-end technology. It appeared to be part of a larger device.

As I examined it closely, my breath caught in my throat. The piece gleamed in the museum's soft lighting, its smooth surface interrupted only by a small etching on one side.

"Mr. Butterfield?" Lily's voice floated up from below, tinged with a mix of worry and excitement. "What is it? What did you find? Is it the egg?"

I took a deep breath, steeling myself for the complications I knew were coming. "It's not the egg," I called down, my voice tight with tension. "But it might be something even more interesting."

Slowly, I descended the ladder, clutching the object carefully. As my feet touched the ground, I held it up for everyone to see. The group clustered around, eyes wide with curiosity.

"This," I said, my voice grave, "is part of a device I wasn't expecting to find here. And it's going to complicate our case significantly."

Dorothy leaned in, squinting at the object. "What is it? Part of some fancy egg timer?"

"Not quite," I replied, turning it so they could all see the etching on its side. "Take a look at this."

There, etched into the side of the device, was a familiar name: NautiluxTech Innovations.

Victor Sterling's company.

Chapter 5

"NautiluxTech Innovations?" Aaron asked. "Jim, do you know something about this company?"

Lily's eyes lit up with recognition. "That name sounds familiar. I think I've heard it before."

I nodded, feeling the weight of the connection settle on my shoulders like a heavy coat. "It's the company owned by Victor Sterling, a businessman who organized the boat racing tournament here last month. They specialize in high-tech devices, including drones."

"Right!" Lily exclaimed. "Now I remember. We saw that company name in the Gazette when we were reading about that case."

Aaron's expression grew serious, his eyes narrowing as he considered the implications. "Do you think Victor could be part of this theft, Jim?"

I shook my head, remembering the last time I'd seen Victor – being led away in handcuffs after our confrontation at the B&B, his expensive suit wrinkled and his usually impeccable hair disheveled. "It's unlikely. Victor is currently enjoying an all-expenses-paid stay at the state prison."

I paused, catching Ginger's gaze. His green eyes were full of understanding, and he gave a slight nod, his tail twitching in what I'd come to recognize as his 'we're onto something' signal. It was time to share my theory.

"Though," I continued, "I do have an idea who might be behind this."

All eyes were on me now, a mix of curiosity and anticipation evident on their faces. Even Josh had stopped fidgeting with his mop, hanging on my every word like I was about to reveal the secret to streak-free window cleaning.

"At the end of our last case, our friend Robert – who had been studying the drones used to sabotage his boat during the race – shared a theory with us. He suggested that Marcus, the champion, might have had an accomplice during the race. Someone who actually controlled the drones from the shore."

"Why would he need an accomplice?" Aaron asked, his brow furrowed in concentration.

"Because it would have been nearly impossible for Marcus to maneuver his boat and control the drones at the same time," I explained, gesturing with my hands to illustrate the point. "It was just too complex an operation for one person to handle alone. Imagine trying to pat your head, rub your stomach, and solve a Rubik's cube all at once – while on a speeding boat."

"Wait," Lily interjected, her eyes widening in recognition. "Is this the same Robert who helped rescue me from the island on his boat?"

I nodded. "The very same."

"A great man," Aaron commented, his voice warm with gratitude.

"Indeed," I agreed. "At the time, we didn't think much of Robert's theory. It was just speculation, and we eventually dropped it. Everyone got busy with their lives, and we forgot about it. But now..." I held up the drone part, its sleek surface glinting in the museum's soft lighting like a high-tech beacon of trouble.

Josh suddenly piped up, his voice cracking with excitement. "So you think the drones could have been used to steal the egg?" His eyes were wide with awe, reminding me of a kid who'd just discovered that Santa Claus was real and happened to be a master thief. "That's so cool! It's like something straight out of a spy movie!"

His enthusiasm dimmed slightly as a thought occurred to him, his face scrunching up in concentration. "But wait, those drones at the race were sea drones. How could they be used in here? Unless... oh my god, do we have indoor pools I don't know about? Have I been missing out on secret museum swimming all this time?"

I turned to Josh, impressed by his observation and slightly concerned about his imagination of secret museum pools. "Good point, Josh. And no, there are no secret pools – though that would certainly liven up the fossil exhibit." I paused, imagining dinosaur bones wearing floaties, before shaking off the absurd mental image. "NautiluxTech Innovations didn't just produce sea drones. They had various types of drones and technology. In fact, I remember reading about their failed military contracts, which means they were producing military-grade tech. The kind of tech that could potentially cut even the strongest glass – like what we see here in the display case."

Dorothy shook her head. "I still can't believe that's even possible. The security measures we have in place... they were supposed to be unbeatable. We might as well have used a cardboard box with 'Please Don't Steal' written on it in crayon."

Lily, her eyes shining with the excitement of piecing together clues, chimed in. "Those drones could be controlled from a distance, right? So the thief probably didn't even need to get inside the room. They could just deploy the drone through the vent system!"

I nodded, impressed by her deduction. "That's possible, but unlikely. Someone still had to put that photograph over the camera and move the 'Cleaning in Progress' sign from the Modern History Room to the Easter Egg Room." I paused, a new thought occurring to me. "Though it's still unclear why the thief would send the drone or whatever device they used back into the vent. If they could have just taken both the egg and the device with them through the front door."

Aaron stroked his chin thoughtfully, looking like a detective from an old noir film. "It probably would have looked suspicious if someone entered the building empty-handed and then left with both a fancy drone and a precious Easter Egg. That's not exactly your typical museum gift shop purchase."

Dorothy nodded vigorously, her glasses slipping down her nose with the motion. She pushed them back up with a practiced move. "I would have definitely spotted something like that. I may be getting on in years, but my eyes are as sharp as ever when it comes to protecting our exhibits. I once caught a kid trying to smuggle out a trilobite fossil in his shoe. Imagine my surprise when I thought I heard the Jurassic period walking by."

A thought struck me, cutting through the amusing image of a fossil-footed child. "Dorothy, where does this vent lead?"

She frowned, her forehead creasing in concentration. "I'm not entirely sure, to be honest. But I assume it leads somewhere outside, probably on an exterior wall. I think I know where it might be."

"Can you take us there?" I asked.

Dorothy nodded, a glint of excitement in her eyes. "Of course. But first..." She turned to Josh, who was still clutching his mop like it was the last lifeboat on the Titanic. "Josh, I need you to stay here and watch the room until the police arrive. Can you do that? And try not to rearrange the crime scene while practicing your mopping choreography."

Josh straightened up, puffing out his chest slightly and nearly poking himself in the eye with the mop handle. "You can count on me, Ms. Collins. I'll guard this room like it's the last roll of toilet paper during a pandemic!"

As the others started to file out of the room, I hung back for a moment, crouching down to Ginger's level. "I need you to do something for me," I whispered, making sure the others couldn't hear. "Can you climb up the ladder and jump into the vent? See if you can spot or smell anything crucial in there. We'll meet you on the other side. And try not to get into a turf war with any museum mice while you're at it."

Ginger's whiskers twitched, his eyes narrowing in a look that could only be described as feline exasperation. "Ah yes, because it's always the cat who has to do the dirty work. Next time, why don't you crawl through the dusty, cramped vent while I lounge comfortably and offer sarcastic commentary? I'm sure you'd fit right in with the dust bunnies. You've already got the color scheme down with that grey in your hair."

Despite his complaints, I watched as Ginger padded over to the ladder, his movements silent and graceful. With a final glance back at me – one that clearly said, "The things I do for you, you overgrown, hairless ape" – he began to climb.

Satisfied that Ginger was on the job, I hurried to catch up with the others. As we stepped outside, the bright spring sunlight was almost jarring after the dim interior of the museum, making me squint like a mole emerging from its burrow.

Dorothy led us around the side of the building, her eyes scanning the exterior wall with the intensity of a prospector searching for gold. "It should be somewhere around here," she muttered, more to herself than to us. "Unless the building decided to rearrange itself when we weren't looking."

We didn't have to search for long. About halfway down the wall, we spotted an open vent cover lying on the ground, the screws that once held it in place scattered in the grass like metallic breadcrumbs.

Aaron let out a low whistle, the sound cutting through the quiet air. "Well, looks like our thief didn't bother closing up after themselves. Not exactly the 'leave no trace' approach, is it?"

I nodded, crouching down to examine the open vent. "They probably didn't think we'd get here so quickly."

As I leaned in closer to the vent, I heard a faint sound coming from inside. It started as a distant rumble but quickly grew louder, accompanied by what sounded suspiciously like feline yowls. It reminded me of the time Ginger had accidentally gotten stuck in the dryer – an incident we had both agreed never to speak of again.

"Do you hear that?" I asked, turning to the others.

Before anyone could respond, I caught sight of an orange blur hurtling toward me from the depths of the vent. I barely had time to jerk my head back before Ginger came flying out, landing squarely on my chest with enough force to knock me backwards onto the grass. For a moment, all I could see was orange fur and all I could hear was Ginger's indignant meows mixed with Lily's laughter.

"What on earth did Ginger do in there?" Lily gasped between giggles. "Was he testing out for the cat Olympics? I think he just set a new record in the furball shot put!"

I managed to sit up, Ginger still perched on my chest like some sort of feline conquering hero. His fur was ruffled, covered in dust, and he had a cobweb delicately draped over one ear like a tiny, silken veil. "Probably... investigating," I wheezed, trying to catch my breath. "Or auditioning for 'Cats: The Action Movie'."

Dorothy shook her head, a mixture of amusement and disbelief on her face. "I've heard rumors about your unusual investigation methods, but I must say, seeing is believing."

Ginger, seemingly satisfied with his dramatic entrance, hopped gracefully off my chest and onto the grass. He began grooming himself with an air of dignified nonchalance.

"You asked me to get in there yourself," Ginger meowed, though of course, only I could understand him. "I didn't realize you wanted me to use you as a landing pad. Next time, perhaps lay out some pillows."

I muttered under my breath as Aaron and Lily helped me to my feet, brushing grass and cat hair from my clothes. "Thanks," I said, plucking a dandelion from my hair.

As I straightened up, I could feel my back protesting the sudden gymnastics it had just been forced to perform. Getting too old for this, I thought ruefully. Maybe it's time to invest in some padding. Or a suit of armor.

"Well," I said, trying to regain some semblance of professional composure, "I think the case is becoming clearer. The thief probably used the drone to enter the room through the vent, cut the hole in the display glass, steal the egg, and then send the drone back out through the vent."

Aaron nodded, his expression thoughtful. "That probably only took a couple of minutes, at most. Talk about efficiency."

"Exactly," I agreed. "But they still had to be inside the museum to put up that 'Cleaning in Progress' sign and make sure no one entered the room while the drone was doing its job. Can't exactly send a drone to hang up a sign. Well, I suppose you could, but that would be showing off." I turned to Dorothy. "We should go to the security room and check the other camera recordings. We might be able to see who entered the museum this morning."

As we made our way back into the museum, I hung back slightly, using the moment to confer quietly with Ginger. "Did you see anything unusual in the vent?"

Ginger shook his head, his whiskers twitching. "Nothing visually interesting, unless you count the fascinating variety of dust bunnies. I think I saw one evolve opposable thumbs. But there was a distinct metallic smell – probably from the drone used to steal the egg. It smelled like a robot's armpit in there."

I nodded, feeling more certain of my theory. The pieces were starting to fall into place, forming a picture that was both exciting and troubling.

As we passed by the restrooms on our way to the security room, Dorothy paused, knocking gently on the door. "Ben? Are you still in there?"

A muffled voice replied from within, sounding strained and slightly embarrassed, "Five more minutes!"

"Looks like he's going for the Mayor's record," Ginger quipped. "Though I'm not sure that's a title anyone should aspire to."

"It's okay," I said to Dorothy. "We can talk to him when he... emerges."

We continued on, passing through the room that preceded the Easter Egg exhibit. Aaron, ever observant, noticed something.

"Look," he said, pointing to a security camera mounted high on the wall. "There's another piece of paper covering that camera. The one that points toward the Easter Egg Room's door."

I nodded, unsurprised. "It was predictable. The thief wouldn't want anyone to see them placing the 'Cleaning in Progress' sign. It would have made it too easy for us to identify them."

Dorothy shook her head, her expression a mix of admiration and frustration. "We must be dealing with a professional. Or at least someone who's watched every heist movie ever made."

"Maybe," I conceded. "But whether they're a professional or not, one thing's for certain – this was all carefully planned. It's not exactly the work of an amateur or someone who decided on a whim to steal a priceless artifact."

We finally reached the security room, where we found a guard hunched over a bank of monitors, his brow furrowed in concentration. He looked up as we entered, his expression a mix of frustration and relief at seeing Dorothy.

Dorothy quickly made introductions. "Everyone, this is Max, our security guard. Max, you probably know Jim Butterfield and Ginger, our local detectives. These are their friends Aaron and Lily, who are helping us find the egg."

Max nodded distractedly, his attention already back on the screens. "I've been checking everything, Ms. Collins, and I can't make heads or tails of it. The camera in the room before the Easter Egg exhibit is just... static. Nothing's happening there at all. It's like watching paint dry, if the paint was invisible and possibly stolen."

Dorothy sighed. "That's because there's another piece of paper with a photograph covering it, just like in the Easter Egg Room."

Max's shoulders slumped. "Well, that's just great. Looks like we're out of luck then. Maybe we should install cameras to watch our cameras."

I stepped forward. "Not necessarily. Can you check the recordings from the museum's entrance? We need to see who was entering and exiting this morning."

Max nodded, his fingers flying over the keyboard as he pulled up the relevant footage. But before he could start playing it, Lily spoke up.

"Wait a second," she said, her voice tinged with excitement. "I just thought of something. In all those spy movies, when there's a robbery in a museum, doesn't an alarm go off when someone breaks the display case? You know, with flashing lights and sirens and possibly some dramatic music?"

Dorothy's eyes widened. "You're absolutely right, dear. We do have an alarm system." She turned to Max. "Why didn't it go off?"

Max's face paled as he began frantically searching through the control panel, mumbling under his breath. His fingers flew over the buttons and switches, and beads of sweat formed on his forehead as he navigated the complex system.

"Come on, come on," he muttered, his eyes darting between screens. "Where is it? It's got to be here somewhere."

We all leaned in, the tension in the room thick enough to cut with a knife. Even Ginger, usually the picture of feline nonchalance, had his ears perked forward in attention.

After what felt like an eternity but was probably only a minute, Max looked up. His expression was a mix of shock, disbelief, and what I can only describe as the face of someone who's just realized they left the stove on... for a week.

"The alarm system," he said, his voice barely above a whisper. "It's... it's turned off."

Chapter 6

The tension in the small security room was palpable as Max's words hung in the air. The alarm system – the supposed last line of defense against theft – had been turned off. I could almost hear the gears turning in everyone's heads as we processed this new information.

Max's face had gone pale, his eyes wide with panic. His fingers trembled as he frantically tapped at the keyboard, double-checking his findings. "I swear, I didn't turn it off!" he exclaimed, his voice cracking slightly. "I would never... I mean, that's basic security protocol!"

I held up a hand, trying to project calm despite the sinking feeling in my stomach. "Easy there, Max. No one's accusing you of anything." I glanced around the room, taking in the worried expressions on everyone's faces. Even Dorothy, usually the picture of composure, looked shaken. "Let's take a step back and think this through logically. Dorothy, who has access to this security room?"

Dorothy straightened her glasses. "Only staff members have access. That would be myself, Max, Josh, and Ben."

I nodded, taking in this new piece of information. "Max, when you leave this room, even for just a couple of minutes, do you always close the door behind you?"

Max nodded vigorously, seemingly relieved to have a simple question to answer. "Always. It's written in the protocol. I never leave it open, not even for a second."

As Max spoke, I felt the familiar weight of a case settling over me. Two possibilities were forming in my mind, neither of them particularly pleasant. Either one of the staff members – Dorothy, Max, Josh, or even the temporarily indisposed Ben – was lying to us, or our thief had somehow gained access to this room. Both options opened up a whole new can of worms.

I pushed these thoughts aside for the moment. We needed more information before we could start pointing fingers or diving down conspiracy rabbit holes. "Alright, let's get back to the front door camera footage," I said, turning to Max. "But first, you might want to turn that alarm system back on. Just in case our egg thief decides they need some accessories to go with their new acquisition."

Max nodded, his shoulders relaxing slightly at having a straightforward task. His fingers flew over the keyboard, and within moments, a soft beep confirmed that the alarm system was once again active. With that done, he pulled up the footage from the front entrance camera.

As Max fast-forwarded through the morning's events, he provided a running commentary. "Here's Ms. Collins arriving," he said, pointing to a figure entering the frame.

"She always comes in first. Then there's Josh for his morning cleaning routine." Another figure appeared. "And here's Ben and me," Max continued as two more figures entered together. "We ran into each other on our way to the museum."

I watched the footage carefully, looking for anything out of the ordinary. So far, everything seemed to match up with what we'd been told. But then, something caught my eye. "Wait," I said, leaning in closer to the screen. "Who's that?"

Max paused the footage, zooming in on two figures entering the museum. They looked young, probably in their early twenties. "Oh, right," he said. "A young couple came in a bit later. Tourists, I think."

My interest piqued. "When did they leave?"

To my surprise, it was Dorothy who answered. "They haven't," she said. "When I went to close the museum, I found them in the Ancient History Room. They're paleontology students, apparently quite fascinated by our dinosaur bones. I didn't tell them about the theft – didn't want to cause a panic. But I did instruct Max to keep an eye on them, just in case."

Max nodded, switching the view to a live feed of the Ancient History Room. Sure enough, there were the two students, bent over a display case, seemingly oblivious to the drama unfolding around them.

"Good thinking," I said, impressed by Dorothy's foresight. "Let's continue with the front door footage. Anyone else come in after them?"

Max fast-forwarded again, but the only other arrivals were our own group. "That's it," he said. "No one else came in, and no one left."

Aaron, who had been quietly observing until now, spoke up. "So, to sum up: the only people who entered the museum today were staff members, that young couple, and us?"

I nodded, mulling over this information. "Seems that way. Unless..." A thought struck me. "Dorothy, are there any emergency exits someone could have used to sneak in?"

Dorothy shook her head. "There are two emergency exits, but I checked them earlier. Both were closed, with no signs of forced entry."

"And there are no cameras on those exits," Max added. "Even if someone did use them, we'd have no way of knowing. Our budget barely covers the existing security measures, let alone additional cameras."

I sighed, running a hand through my hair. "Well, looks like we've got another locked-room mystery on our hands. Unless our thief really did use that drone for everything – moving the 'Cleaning in Progress' sign, attaching those fake photos to the camera lenses..."

"Or someone here isn't telling the whole truth," Aaron finished, his voice low.

The tension in the room skyrocketed at Aaron's words. I could almost feel the suspicion crackling in the air like static electricity. Dorothy opened her mouth, likely to protest, but before she could speak, the distant wail of police sirens cut through the silence.

Dorothy's shoulders sagged with relief. "That'll be the police," she said. "I should go let them in." With that, she hurried out of the room, leaving us in an uncomfortable silence.

I turned to Max, aware that our time was running short. "Listen, Max. Knowing Sheriff Miller, he'll probably want to clear the building as soon as he arrives. If you remember anything unusual from this morning's events – anything at all – give me a call." I pulled a business card out of my wallet and handed it to him. "Day or night, doesn't matter."

Max took the card, nodding solemnly. "Will do, Mr. Butterfield. And don't worry – we'll catch whoever did this. No one steals from my museum and gets away with it."

As we left the security room, Lily's eyes were shining with excitement. "That was so cool, Mr. Butterfield!" she exclaimed. "You're like a real detective from those mystery movies!"

"Someone's got to solve these mysteries," I said with a shrug. "Especially with the, ah, unique brand of law enforcement we have in this town."

As if on cue, we rounded a corner to see Sheriff Miller and his team entering the museum. Miller was in the lead, his considerable bulk filling the doorway as he stepped inside. Behind him, Officers Murphy, Martinez, and Jones fanned out, their hands hovering near their holsters as if expecting the egg thief to jump out from behind a stuffed mammoth at any moment.

"Well, well," Ginger muttered. "If it isn't Oceanview Cove's finest. Quite the dream team we've got here. Like the local Avengers, if the Avengers were more interested in donuts than saving the world."

I stifled a laugh as Miller's gaze landed on us. His bushy eyebrows furrowed, creating a look of perpetual confusion that I'd come to associate with his attempts at detective work.

"Butterfield," he grunted, his mustache twitching like an agitated caterpillar. "Why is it that whenever there's trouble in this town, you and that cat of yours are always nearby?"

I plastered on my best innocent smile. "Just lucky, I guess. Always happy to see you too, Sheriff."

Miller's gaze shifted to Aaron and Lily, recognition dawning in his eyes. "And you two," he said, his frown deepening. "Thought after that adventure last year, you'd have the good sense to stay as far away from this town as possible."

Lily grinned, seemingly unfazed by Miller's gruff demeanor. "Guess we just can't resist a good mystery, Sheriff."

Miller harrumphed, his mustache quivering with disapproval. "Alright, Butterfield," he said, turning back to me. "Fill me in on what's going on here before the actual professionals get to work." He gestured vaguely at his team, who were currently engaged in what appeared to be a heated debate over whether dinosaurs could have stolen the egg.

I raised an eyebrow. "Are you asking for my help, Sheriff? I'm touched."

Miller's face reddened slightly. "Don't get ahead of yourself," he growled. "I just need to make sure you and your little detective club aren't the ones who actually stole the egg."

"Ah yes," Ginger meowed sarcastically, "because nothing says 'master criminals' like a retired librarian, a feline genius with impeccable investigative skills, and two tourists. We're clearly Ocean's Eleven material."

Suppressing a smile at Ginger's self-praise, I nodded at Miller. "Fair enough. We'll tell you everything we know. But first, you might want to send some officers to check on those paleontology students in the Ancient History Room. Just to be thorough."

Miller considered this for a moment, then nodded. "Murphy, Jones," he barked. "Go check out these students. Martinez, set up a police line at the front door. No one in or out without my say-so."

As his officers scurried to follow orders, Miller turned back to me. "Alright, Butterfield. Start talking."

I took a deep breath and launched into our tale, starting from the moment we entered the museum. I was just getting to the part about discovering the empty display case when Murphy and Jones returned, escorting the two paleontology students.

The students looked bewildered, their eyes wide as they took in the scene. The young man, his glasses slightly askew, kept glancing between Miller and me as if trying to decide who was actually in charge. The woman walked stiffly beside him, her arms crossed tightly over her chest, fingers digging into her sleeves.

"What should we do with them, Sheriff?" Jones asked, looking entirely too pleased with himself for having successfully escorted two confused college students across a museum.

Miller's eyes narrowed as he studied the pair. "Search them," he ordered gruffly.

What followed was a scene that would have been at home in a slapstick comedy. Murphy, apparently under the impression that a Fabergé egg could be concealed in a wallet, began methodically removing every card and receipt from the young man's billfold. Jones, meanwhile, seemed convinced that the egg might be hiding in the woman's hair, and was carefully patting her head as if expecting a golden egg to suddenly pop out from her ponytail.

Ginger's whiskers twitched in amusement. "Jim," he meowed quietly, "please remind me never to complain about your investigative methods again. At least you've never tried to solve a case by giving someone a surprise haircut."

After several minutes of increasingly ridiculous searching, Murphy and Jones were forced to admit defeat. The egg was nowhere to be found on the students.

The young man, his hair now sticking up at odd angles thanks to Jones's thorough investigation, fixed Miller with an indignant glare. "Are you quite finished?" he asked, his voice dripping with sarcasm. "Or would you like to check our teeth next? I hear ancient Egyptians used to hide treasures in hollow molars."

Miller, looking slightly deflated, waved a hand dismissively. "You two, stay put. I'll be interviewing you later." He turned back to me, his mustache drooping slightly. "Alright, Butterfield. Continue."

I picked up where I'd left off, filling Miller in on everything we'd discovered, including the drone part we'd found in the vent. As I handed over the small piece of technology, I could almost see the gears turning in Miller's head – probably trying to remember if he'd ever seen a drone that wasn't delivering pizzas.

"So," Miller said slowly once I'd finished, "any suspects?"

I shrugged. "Well, unless you believe in invisible thieves who can walk through walls, I'd say our suspect pool is limited to the museum staff or someone with inside knowledge of the security systems."

Dorothy, who had been hovering nearby, looked stricken. "I simply can't believe anyone on my staff would do such a thing," she protested.

Miller nodded, his expression serious. "We'll be interviewing everyone here," he said. Then, turning to me, he added, "You and your friends are free to go for now, Butterfield. The professionals will take it from here." He emphasized the word 'professionals' with a pointed look. "And I don't want to hear about any amateur detective work around here. The museum is now a sealed crime scene."

I held up my hands in mock surrender. "When have Ginger and I ever violated police orders, Sheriff?"

"I could name a few occasions," Ginger muttered. "Though I doubt Miller has enough fingers to count them all."

I turned to Dorothy, pulling a business card from my wallet. "If you notice anything strange about the staff's behavior or think of anything else that might be helpful, give me a call," I said, handing her the card.

Dorothy took the card, a grateful smile breaking through her worried expression. "Thank you all so much," she said, her gaze sweeping over our little group. "I truly appreciate your help in this difficult situation."

***

As we made our way out of the museum, we were treated to the sight of Martinez struggling with the police tape. He had somehow managed to tangle himself up, creating what looked like a modern art installation titled "Officer in Distress."

"I don't think it works like that," Ginger observed dryly. "Unless the plan is to mummify any potential suspects."

Once we were outside, Lily turned to me. "Do you think the police can actually find the thief?" she asked.

Aaron snorted. "The chances of that are zero point zero."

I nodded in agreement. "They're more likely to arrest those poor students for looking suspicious than to find the real culprit."

Lily's face set in a determined expression that reminded me startlingly of her father. "Then it's up to us," she declared. "We have to find the egg, just like Emma predicted. We're going to fix everything."

I couldn't help but smile at her enthusiasm. It was refreshing, especially given the gravity of the situation. "Alright, team," I said, feeling a bit like a coach giving a pep talk. "We need a plan."

Aaron raised an eyebrow. "I assume you have one?"

I nodded, the beginnings of an idea forming in my mind. "Ginger and I need to check something out first,"

I said. "Meanwhile, I need you two to do some digging. Find out everything you can about that egg – its value, any previous attempts to steal it, anything that might be relevant. Also, see what you can learn from the townsfolk at the Easter Fair. In a place like Oceanview Cove, someone always knows something. And with Mrs. Henderson's gossip ring in full swing, I'd bet half the town already knows about the stolen egg."

Lily nodded eagerly, already pulling out her phone to take notes. "Where should we meet to share what we've learned?"

"Let's meet at the Salty Breeze this evening," I suggested. "Shawn, Emma, and Robert will be there too. We can review everything we've discovered and plan our next move."

"Sounds good," Aaron agreed. "But where are you and Ginger headed?"

I exchanged a glance with Ginger, seeing my own determination reflected in his green eyes. "We're going to pay a visit to our old friend Victor Sterling," I said. "I think it's time we got some answers about those drones."

Chapter 7

The state prison loomed before us, a stark contrast to the scenic coastal drive we'd just completed. Unlike the grim, industrial facility where Maggie was incarcerated, this prison had an almost collegiate air about it. The buildings were red brick with white trim, set amidst manicured lawns and neatly pruned trees. If it weren't for the imposing security fences topped with razor wire, one might mistake it for an exclusive private school.

I eased my old Buick into a parking spot, the engine sputtering slightly before falling silent. "Well, here we are," I said, turning to Ginger. "Victor's new home."

Ginger stretched lazily in the passenger seat. "Quite the upgrade from Oceanview Cove's police station, isn't it? I suppose money talks, even behind bars."

I nodded, remembering the brief stint Victor had spent in the holding cell before his lawyer had worked some legal magic. "His attorney must be worth every penny of those exorbitant fees. This place looks more like a country club than a prison."

"So," Ginger said, fixing me with his piercing green gaze, "I assume you want me to wait out here while you go in for your little chat with our favorite incarcerated tech mogul?"

"That's the plan," I confirmed. "Just like last time with Maggie."

Ginger's whiskers twitched with amusement. "Tell me, Jim, why exactly did I need to come along on this little road trip? I could be at home right now, enjoying a delightful nap in that sunny spot by the window."

I couldn't help but smile at his grumbling. "Come now, partner. It's all part of the job. Besides, it was a long drive. I would've been bored out of my mind without your sparkling conversation."

"Oh, of course," Ginger replied, his voice dripping with sarcasm. "Heaven forbid you be left alone with your thoughts for a few hours. Though I must say, I'm impressed this ancient chariot of yours made it here in one piece. I half expected us to break down halfway and have to hitch a ride on the back of a passing tractor."

I patted the dashboard affectionately. "Don't listen to him, old girl. You did just fine."

Ginger rolled his eyes. "Wonderful. Now you're talking to the car. Clearly, this investigation is addling what's left of your wits." He paused, tilting his head curiously. "Speaking of the investigation, what exactly do you hope to get out of Victor? It's not as if he can shed much light on our egg thief from behind bars."

In response, I pulled out my smartphone and pulled up a photo I'd taken earlier. It showed the series number etched onto the piece of drone we'd found in the museum vent. Ginger's eyes widened in surprise.

"When did you take that?" he asked, genuine astonishment in his voice. "And more importantly, how did you manage to operate the camera without accidentally booking yourself a yoga class?"

I couldn't help but feel a bit smug. "What can I say? My technological skills are improving. I actually sent an email attachment on the first try last week."

"Miracles never cease," Ginger muttered. "Though I doubt the guards will let you take that phone inside."

"You're right," I agreed, pocketing the phone. "That's why I've memorized the series number. I'm going to ask Victor about this specific drone and who might have access to it."

Ginger nodded approvingly. "Not bad, old man. There might be hope for you yet." He stretched again. "Well, while you're in there playing twenty questions with our imprisoned nemesis, I suppose I'll do a bit of investigating myself. This perimeter won't patrol itself, after all."

We got out of the car, the gravel crunching under my feet while Ginger landed silently beside me. The air was cooler here than back in Oceanview Cove, carrying a hint of pine from the nearby forest. A red-tailed hawk circled lazily overhead, its cry echoing across the parking lot.

"Good luck in there," Ginger said, his tail swishing behind him. "Try not to let Victor get under your skin. And if he offers you any prison cuisine, politely decline. I've heard the mystery meat is particularly mysterious."

I chuckled, giving Ginger a final scratch behind the ears before heading toward the entrance. The guard station was a small, fortified building separate from the main prison. As I approached, a burly guard with a neatly trimmed mustache eyed me warily.

"Purpose of visit?" he asked, his voice gruff and businesslike.

"I'm here to see Victor Sterling," I replied, trying to project confidence. "Jim Butterfield, private investigator."

The guard's eyebrows rose slightly. "Sterling? He's not accepting visitors except for his lawyer." He picked up a phone, dialing a number. "Let me check with inside."

As the guard spoke in low tones into the phone, I found myself fidgeting nervously. What if Victor refused to see me? This whole trip would have been for nothing.

The guard's conversation seemed to stretch on endlessly. Finally, he hung up the phone. "Surprisingly, Sterling's agreed to see you," he said, sounding as shocked as I felt. "Head on in."

I nodded, relieved and a bit apprehensive. What had made Victor change his mind? As I followed the guard's directions, I couldn't shake the feeling that I was walking into something more complicated than I'd anticipated.

The security procedures were familiar by now, though no less tedious. I emptied my pockets, went through the metal detector, and endured the pat-down with as much dignity as I could muster. Finally, with a visitor's badge clipped to my shirt, I was led to the visiting room.

Unlike the grim, concrete visiting area where I'd met Maggie, this room had an almost cheerful air about it. The walls were painted a soft blue, and there were even a few potted plants scattered around, their green leaves a welcome splash of color in the otherwise sterile environment.

A guard directed me to a table near the center of the room. As I sat on the uncomfortable plastic chair, I noticed the security cameras mounted in each corner, their red lights blinking steadily. Armed guards stood at regular intervals along the walls, their expressions neutral but alert.

The minutes ticked by slowly. Then the door on the opposite side of the room opened, and Victor Sterling walked in.

If I had expected prison to have humbled him, I would have been sorely disappointed. Victor strode into the room with the same confidence he'd displayed at the boat race, his head held high and his back ramrod straight. The orange jumpsuit, which looked baggy and unflattering on most inmates, somehow managed to look tailored on him.

"Butterfield," he said as he sat down across from me, his voice carrying that same smooth charm it had when he'd first hired me to find the prize money. "What an unexpected pleasure. I must admit, I was intrigued when the guard told me you were here."

I studied his face carefully, looking for any cracks in his polished facade. "Hello, Victor. You're looking... well."

A small smile played at the corners of his mouth. "Prison life agrees with me, it seems. However, the accommodations leave something to be desired." His eyes met mine, sharp and calculating. "But surely you didn't drive all this way to discuss prison decor. What brings Oceanview Cove's finest detective to my humble abode?"

I leaned forward slightly, keeping my voice low. "I need information, Victor. About your company, specifically about a certain type of drone."

Victor's eyebrows rose fractionally, the only indication that my words had caught him off guard. "Drones? Come now, Jim. Surely there are more pressing matters to discuss. How's the charming town of Oceanview Cove?"

"Cut the small talk, Victor," I said, my patience wearing thin. "A drone was used in a theft. A theft of a very valuable artifact from our museum."

Now Victor did look surprised, though whether it was genuine or not, I couldn't tell. "A theft? How exciting. Do tell me more."

I gave him a brief rundown of the Easter Egg theft, watching his reactions carefully. As I spoke, his expression shifted from mild amusement to genuine interest.

"Fascinating," he said when I'd finished. "A real mystery on your hands. But I fail to see what this has to do with me or my company. In case you haven't noticed, I'm not exactly in a position to be orchestrating high-tech heists."

I recited the series number from the drone part. "This number was found on a piece of technology at the crime scene. It matches the serial numbers used by NautiluxTech Innovations."

Victor's eyes widened almost imperceptibly as he heard the number. For a moment, his carefully maintained mask slipped, revealing a mix of recognition and what might have been concern. But it was gone in an instant, replaced by his usual smooth demeanor.

"Ah," he said, leaning back in his chair. "Now that is interesting. That is the serial number for one of our more... experimental projects."

"What kind of project?" I pressed.

Victor's eyes gleamed with what might have been pride. "We called it the Spider Drone. Quite the marvel of engineering, if I do say so myself. It could crawl like a spider, you see, with legs that could grip almost any surface. And it was equipped with cutting tools that could slice through even the strongest materials."

I thought of the neat circular cut in the museum's reinforced glass. "What happened to these drones? Why haven't I heard of them before?"

Victor waved a hand dismissively. "Ah, well, the military wasn't interested. They wanted things that could fly or swim, not crawl. Shortsighted, if you ask me. We only made a handful of prototypes before the project was scrapped."

"And what happened to those prototypes?" I asked, leaning forward intently.

Victor's smile turned slightly predatory. "Now that, Butterfield, is the interesting question, isn't it? Tell me, how badly do you want to know?"

I gritted my teeth, knowing I was walking into some sort of trap but seeing no way around it. "What do you want, Victor?"

"Information for information," he said smoothly. "You tell me everything you know about this theft, every detail, and I'll tell you what happened to those drones."

I hesitated, weighing my options. On one hand, sharing details of an ongoing investigation with Victor felt wrong on multiple levels. On the other, this might be our only lead to finding the egg thief. Finally, I nodded. "Deal."

I laid out everything we knew about the case – the method of entry, the disabled alarms, the photographs covering security cameras. Victor listened intently, occasionally asking pointed questions that made me realize just how sharp his mind was, even behind bars.

When I finished, Victor nodded thoughtfully. "A professional job, no doubt about it. Your thief knows what they're doing." He leaned forward, lowering his voice. "As for the drones, well... when the project was scrapped, I didn't want that technology going to waste. So I had a couple of my more... entrepreneurial employees sell them on the black market. Fetched a tidy sum, too."

I felt my heart sink. If the drones had been sold on the black market, there was no telling where they might have ended up. "Do you remember who you tasked with selling them?"

Victor's brow furrowed in thought. "It was years ago, but... ah, yes. Two friends, brilliant engineers but absolute pains to work with. Aiden Wright and Ethan Zhao. I had to fire them eventually – too many conflicts with other team members. But they knew the tech inside and out, so I figured they were the best choice to handle the sale."

I made a mental note of the names, already formulating plans to track them down. "Anything else you can tell me about them?"

Victor shrugged. "Not much. They were close, those two. Always together, finishing each other's sentences. Brilliant minds, but difficult personalities."

I nodded, feeling like we'd finally made a breakthrough in the case. But there was still one more thing I needed to ask. "Victor, there's a theory I'd like to run by you. It's about the race and Marcus."

Victor leaned back, a hint of amusement in his eyes. "Oh? And here I thought you couldn't surprise me anymore, Butterfield. Do tell."

I explained Robert's theory about the drones and the possibility of a remote operator. "You know as well as I do that these drones have small cameras and are capable of being controlled from a distance. But here's the interesting part – we didn't find any remote controls on Marcus's boat. It got us thinking – what if there was another accomplice? Someone on the coast, controlling the drones remotely while Marcus piloted the boat?"

As I spoke, I watched Victor's face carefully. His expression shifted from mild interest to genuine surprise, and then to something that looked almost like admiration.

"Well, well," he said, stroking his chin thoughtfully. "I must say, I'm impressed. That's quite a clever theory."

"So you didn't know about this?" I pressed. "There was no mention of a third party in your agreement with Marcus."

Victor shook his head, a wry smile playing at his lips. "I only made an agreement with Marcus. Who he hired to help him was his own business. I preferred to keep my hands clean of the details, you understand." His smile turned cold. "And unfortunately, as you well know, Marcus is dead. So there's no way to ask him about it now, is there?"

I suppressed a shiver at his casual mention of Marcus's death. "Well, Victor, I appreciate the information you've shared. I think I've learned all I can from you for now. Thanks for the names of your former engineers. They could be valuable leads."

Victor's smile didn't reach his eyes. "Don't thank me yet, Butterfield. You see, just because I've shared some useful information doesn't mean our little feud is over. I told you what I know because I want to find out who's using my technology myself. Call it… professional curiosity."

"What are you saying, Victor?"

He leaned forward, his voice dropping to a near whisper. "I'm saying that when I get out of here – and make no mistake, I will get out – I'll be coming for you, Jim. You and that feline partner of yours. You cost me everything, and I don't forget things like that."

I tried to keep my voice steady, not wanting to show how his words had affected me. "You'll be in here for a long time, Victor. By the time you get out, I'll probably be with my Martha."

Victor's laugh was cold and humorless. "We'll see about that, won't we? Time has a way of passing quickly, especially when one has… motivation."

Before I could respond, a guard approached our table. "Time's up," he announced gruffly.

Victor stood, smoothing down his jumpsuit. "Well, this has been delightful, Butterfield. Do give my regards to everyone in Oceanview Cove."

As he was led away, Victor turned back for a moment, his eyes meeting mine. The look in them sent a chill through me – it was the look of a predator, patient and calculating, willing to wait as long as necessary for its prey.

The exit procedure was mercifully quick, and before I knew it, I was back in the bright sunlight of the parking lot. As my eyes adjusted, I spotted a familiar orange form sprawled across the hood of my car.

"Well, well," I said as I approached, "I see your perimeter investigation was thorough. Did you check for escape tunnels under my hubcaps?"

Ginger stretched lazily. "I'll have you know I conducted a comprehensive security assessment," he replied. "I've determined that the squirrels in that oak tree over there are highly suspicious and potentially in league with our egg thief."

I chuckled as I unlocked the car, gesturing for Ginger to hop inside. "I'm sure they are. Probably planning a nut heist as we speak."

As we settled into our seats, Ginger fixed me with his piercing green gaze. "So, how was your chat with our imprisoned tech tycoon? Did he spill any useful beans, or was it just an hour of thinly veiled threats and reminiscing about his glory days?"

I started the engine, which sputtered to life with its usual reluctance. As we pulled out of the parking lot, I filled Ginger in on my conversation with Victor, detailing the information about the Spider Drones and the two engineers who might have sold them.

"Aiden Wright and Ethan Zhao," Ginger mused. "Sounds like the beginning of a bad tech startup joke. 'Two difficult engineers walk into a black market sale...'"

"It's our best lead so far," I said, keeping my eyes on the road as we merged onto the highway. "If we can track them down, we might be able to figure out who bought those drones."

"And Victor's threat?" Ginger asked, his tone more serious now. "Do you think he meant it?"

I sighed, remembering the cold look in Victor's eyes. "I don't know. Part of me wants to dismiss it as empty words from a man facing years behind bars. But Victor's not the type to make idle threats. We'll need to be careful."

Chapter 8

The evening sky was a turbulent canvas of dark grays and purples as Ginger and I pulled up to the Salty Breeze. The wind had picked up considerably during our drive back from the prison, whipping the trees into a frenzy and sending loose debris skittering across the road. As I cut the engine, the old Buick gave a shudder of relief, as if grateful for the respite from battling the elements.

"Looks like Robert wasn't exaggerating about that storm," I muttered, peering through the windshield as ominous clouds gathered on the horizon. The air felt heavy with the promise of rain, and the faint rumble of distant thunder made my skin prickle.

Ginger stretched lazily in the passenger seat. "I do hope you're not planning on using this weather as an excuse to avoid sharing what you learned from Victor," he said. "Though I suppose 'sorry, couldn't make it, my car was swept away by a tornado' does have a certain dramatic flair."

I chuckled as I opened the car door, bracing myself against the gust of wind that immediately assaulted us.

"No such luck, I'm afraid. Besides, I already called Aaron on the way back. Everyone's waiting for us inside."

As we approached the bar, the muffled sounds of conversation and laughter drifted out to meet us. It was louder than usual for this time of evening, the normal laid-back atmosphere replaced by something more charged and excited. I pushed open the door, and a wave of warm air rushed out to greet us, carrying with it the familiar scents of beer, fried food, and the underlying mustiness that seemed to be a permanent feature of the Salty Breeze.

The bar was packed, with every table occupied and patrons crowding three rows deep at the counter. The chatter was a constant buzz, punctuated by occasional bursts of laughter or exclamations. As Ginger and I made our way through the throng, I caught snatches of conversation, most of it centered around the day's events.

"...heard it was worth millions..."

"...probably those art thieves from Europe..."

"...bet it was aliens. You know how they love shiny things..."

I shook my head, marveling at the speed with which news – and wild speculation – traveled in our little town. Mrs. Henderson's gossip network was clearly working overtime.

We finally reached the bar, where I spotted our friends gathered around a table. Shawn was behind the counter, expertly mixing drinks while keeping up a steady stream of conversation. His hands moved with practiced ease, pouring and shaking with a rhythm that was almost hypnotic. Robert, Emma, Aaron, and Lily were seated around the table, all leaning in close as if sharing secrets.

As we approached, Shawn looked up and grinned, his eyes twinkling with amusement. "Look who finally made it," he called out over the din. "I was starting to think you'd been swept away by the storm."

"Not for lack of trying," I replied, sliding onto an empty stool. Ginger leapt up gracefully beside me, earning a few curious glances from nearby patrons. "I swear, this town can't have a normal holiday without some kind of mystery cropping up."

Shawn nodded sagely as he wiped down a glass, the cloth squeaking against the surface. "Ain't that the truth. What'll it be, Jim? The usual?"

I shook my head. "Something non-alcoholic tonight, if you don't mind. That cocktail you whipped up at the fair was pretty good. Besides," I added with a wry smile, "I need to keep a clear head. This case is turning out to be more complicated than I thought."

"One Salty Sunset coming right up," Shawn said with a wink. He turned to Ginger. "And for you, sir? The usual cream, I presume?"

Ginger meowed, and I nodded. "You know him well, Shawn."

As Shawn prepared my drink, Aaron leaned in, the excitement clear in his voice. "We were just talking about the case," he said, his eyes bright. "Did you learn anything useful from Victor?"

Before I could answer, Emma chimed in, her crystals tinkling as she gestured dramatically. "It's all just as I predicted, you know. The stars never lie!"

"Is that so?" I replied, amused. "Well, maybe you can tell us who stole the egg then, and save us all a lot of trouble."

Emma's face fell slightly. "Well, no... the stars haven't revealed that particular detail yet. But I'm planning a moonlit stroll on the beach tonight to commune with the celestial energies. I'm sure they'll provide some insight!"

Robert, who had been quietly nursing a beer, spoke up. "I wouldn't advise any beach walks tonight, Emma. There's a hell of a storm brewing out there. I barely made it back from fishing today – it's already getting pretty messy out on the water."

I nodded in agreement, remembering our harrowing drive. "We noticed on the drive back. I thought the car was going to take flight a couple of times."

"Ah yes," Ginger meowed sarcastically, his tail swishing with amusement. "I believe we were about to test the world's first feline-operated flying car. I was looking forward to getting my pilot's license."

I stifled a chuckle and turned to Robert. "How did the fishing go, by the way?"

Robert shrugged, his face creasing into a smile. "Not bad, got what I needed. Though I think my new GPS radar might be on the fritz. It showed a pretty big ship not far from here. Been a while since I've seen anything that size in these waters. Makes me wonder if it's even real – how it'll survive this storm and all."

Shawn, who had returned with our drinks, set them down carefully. The glasses clinked softly against the worn wood of the bar. "I don't trust all this modern technology," he said, shaking his head. "Give me a good old-fashioned compass and a star chart any day."

Emma nodded enthusiastically. "Exactly! The stars have guided sailors for centuries. Why change what works?"

"And yet," Robert mused, taking a sip of his beer, "one of those modern technologies was used to steal the Easter Egg from the museum."

I nodded, taking a sip of my drink. The fruity concoction was just as good as I remembered from the Fair, with a perfect balance of sweet and tart. "Speaking of which, Robert, your theory about Marcus having an accomplice? It's looking more and more likely."

All eyes turned to me as I recounted my conversation with Victor, detailing what I'd learned about the Spider Drones and the two engineers who might have sold them on the black market. The group listened intently, their expressions a mix of fascination and concern.

When I finished, Robert sat back, a look of vindication on his face. "I knew it," he said, thumping his fist on the table. "I knew there had to be more to it than just Marcus."

"And now," I said, leaning forward, my voice low and serious, "we need to catch the thief. It's likely the same person who helped Marcus win the race." I turned to Lily and Aaron. "Did you manage to find out anything about the egg or previous theft attempts?"

Lily's eyes lit up with excitement, reminding me of a child on Christmas morning. "Oh, you wouldn't believe what we found out about the egg! It's got such an amazing history!"

"So, we did some research online, and it all matches up with what Ms. Collins at the museum told us earlier. The egg was found during an archaeological dig just outside town on Easter Sunday a decade ago, and it dates back to the early 18th century."

Lily continued, her hands gesturing animatedly. "Apparently, it was commissioned by a wealthy merchant named Cornelius Hawkins for his wife, Elizabeth. The theory is that it was created by a master craftsman from Europe, though no one knows exactly who."

Her eyes sparkled as she went on. "The craftsmanship is incredible. It's solid gold, covered in diamonds, rubies, and sapphires. There are even tiny pearls that form a delicate floral pattern around the base. And the coolest part? It has these intricate mechanisms inside that make parts of it move when you turn it just right!"

She leaned back, clearly pleased with her storytelling. "Oh, and get this," Lily said, her voice dropping to a dramatic whisper, "it's estimated to be worth over two million dollars!"

I let out a low whistle, the sound almost lost in the general noise of the bar. "No wonder the thief went to all the trouble of getting that fancy drone. The return on investment is huge."

Aaron nodded, his expression thoughtful. "We tried to find information about previous theft attempts, but there wasn't anything online."

Shawn, who had been listening while serving other customers, chimed in. He leaned on the bar, his voice low as if sharing a secret. "That's because the Gazette didn't have a website when the egg was first brought to the museum. There were a couple of attempts to steal it in the first month – though 'steal' might be exaggerating."

He leaned in conspiratorially, his eyes darting around as if checking for eavesdroppers. "It was just some school kids on a museum visit who decided to test the display case's endurance. The alarm went off, and the police responded a couple of times. After that, Miller ordered a 'Do Not Touch' sign to be put up. There haven't been any attempts since then... until now, that is."

Aaron sighed, running a hand through his hair. The gesture spoke volumes about his frustration. "So we're at a dead end, then? What's the next move?"

I glanced out the window, where the wind was now howling, bending trees and sending loose papers swirling through the air like confetti. "For now, I think we should all head home and get some rest. This storm's only going to get worse. Aaron, Lily, I'll give you a lift back to the B&B...

assuming my car doesn't decide to become airborne on the way."

Lily's eyes lit up at that, a mischievous grin spreading across her face. "Even if it does fly away, that would be so cool! Just like Harry Potter!"

"Let's hope it doesn't come to that," I said, shaking my head. "As for tomorrow, we need to track down those engineers Victor mentioned and find out who bought the drones. We should also look into the museum staff, especially that security guard, Ben. It's awfully convenient that he was indisposed during the entire theft."

Shawn nodded, his expression serious. "Just like Mayor Thompson during the Valentine's Day poisoning. Missed all the chaos."

"Right," I agreed, remembering that chaotic day, "but Thompson was also a victim. What happened to Ben is still a mystery."

We spent a few more minutes discussing our plans for the following day. Shawn offered to keep an ear out for any useful information among the patrons' wild theories. Emma, of course, promised to consult the stars, though I gently reminded her not to stay out too late in the storm.

As we wrapped up our discussion, a thought struck me. "You know," I said slowly, "it's awfully suspicious that on the very day the egg is stolen from the museum, a mysterious ship appears in nearby waters. Robert, once this storm clears up, could you ask around the docks and see if anyone else spotted that ship you saw on your radar? It might be nothing, but in this town, coincidences are rarely just coincidences."

Robert nodded, his expression serious. "Will do, Jim. As soon as it's safe to head out, I'll see what I can find out."

We said our goodbyes and made our way toward the exit, navigating through the still-crowded bar. The noise level had increased, if that was possible, and I had to raise my voice to be heard over the din.

As we passed Chuck's table, he called out, his voice slightly slurred from one too many of Shawn's special brews. "Don't brush off that theory about international art thieves, Jim! They could be right here in Oceanview Cove, you know!"

I smiled and promised to keep an open mind, but inwardly, I was certain it wasn't the case. Or was I? Could there really be international art thieves in our little coastal town?

Chapter 9

The shrill beeping of my alarm clock pierced through the peaceful silence of early morning, jolting me awake. I groaned and buried my face deeper into my pillow, hoping against hope that if I ignored it long enough, the infernal noise would simply give up and go away.

No such luck.

"Rise and shine, old man," came Ginger's all-too-chipper voice from somewhere near my feet. "Time for our morning run."

I cracked open one bleary eye to glare at him. The cat was already wide awake, his tail swishing back and forth with anticipation. Outside, I could hear the wind howling, rattling the windows in their frames with an intensity that made me wonder if we were in for an impromptu remodeling.

"Are you out of your mind?" I mumbled, my voice still thick with sleep. "Running in that storm?"

Ginger padded over to the window, peering out at the turbulent sky. His whiskers twitched as a particularly violent gust shook the house. "Hmm, you may have a point there," he conceded. "It would be more of a morning flight than a morning run. But nevertheless, we have to do this. Can't let a little wind deter us from our fitness goals."

I sat up with a groan that seemed to echo through every joint in my body, rubbing the sleep from my eyes. "Look, Ginger, we're in the middle of a case here. Don't you think we should take a break from running until we find the egg?"

Ginger fixed me with an unimpressed stare, his green eyes narrowing. "We only started running yesterday, and you already want to skip a day? Your commitment to fitness is truly inspiring, Jim. Perhaps we should inform the Olympic committee of your rigorous training regimen."

I opened my mouth to argue, to explain the unique circumstances we found ourselves in, but the resolute look in Ginger's eyes told me it would be futile. Instead, I changed tack. "How about we negotiate a day off from running? What would it take? A catnip mouse? A new scratching post? The deed to the house?"

Ginger visibly perked up at this, lifting a paw to his chin in an eerily human-like gesture of contemplation. After a brief pause that seemed designed purely for dramatic effect, he spoke. "That premium cat food you've been saving for a special moment might just break the deal. I'd say this qualifies as a special moment, wouldn't you? Unless, of course, you'd prefer to test your wind resistance out there."

Relief washed over me like a warm shower. "Fine," I agreed, already swinging my legs out of bed. "You drive a hard bargain, but it's a deal."

After a quick shower that did wonders to wash away the last vestiges of sleep, I made my way to the kitchen, the aroma of brewing coffee already filling the air. Ginger had evidently been busy, his coffee-making skills once again putting my fumbling attempts to shame.

"Mind finishing up the coffee while I check the mail?" I asked, eyeing the tempest outside warily. "If our mailbox hasn't flown away to the moon, that is."

"Your lack of faith in your own property is amusing," Ginger replied. "Go on, I'll have your caffeine ready when you return. Assuming you don't get swept away yourself, of course. Though that might solve our morning exercise dilemma."

Bracing myself, I opened the front door and stepped out into chaos. The wind hit me like a physical force, nearly knocking me off balance. Debris littered the street – branches, leaves, and what looked suspiciously like someone's garden gnome tumbling past, its cheery painted smile at odds with its predicament. But there, stalwart as ever, stood our mailbox.

"You'll outlive us all, won't you?" I muttered as I approached it, my words whipped away by the wind. "Probably survive the apocalypse too."

To my surprise, nestled inside was a fresh copy of the Oceanview Cove Gazette. I snatched it up quickly, marveling at the dedication (or perhaps insanity) of our local paperboy.

Back in the warmth of the kitchen, I was greeted by the heavenly aroma of freshly brewed coffee. I took a grateful sip, feeling the caffeine work its magic, chasing away the last cobwebs of sleep and storm-induced bewilderment.

"Once again, you've outdone yourself," I said to Ginger, who was watching me expectantly, his tail curled neatly around his paws. "I don't know how you do it, but this is perfect."

"Naturally," he replied, his whiskers twitching with satisfaction. "Some of us have talents beyond chasing criminals and tripping over clues. Now, what news does our intrepid delivery person bring us today? Any reports of flying cows or houses landing on wicked witches?"

I held up the newspaper, its bold headline practically shouting from the page: "EASTER EGG-STRAVAGANZA: PRICELESS ARTIFACT STOLEN FROM MUSEUM!" The subheading read: "Town in Shock as Centuries-Old Treasure Vanishes – Aliens, International Art Thieves, or Local Mischief?"

"Seems our local newshounds thought it more important to deliver the latest gossip than to stay safely at home," I mused, skimming the article. "Though I have to admire their commitment to keeping the town informed. Or their dedication to wild speculation, at least."

Ginger snorted, a sound that somehow managed to convey both amusement and disdain. "Are you really surprised? In this town, keeping the rumor mill grinding is probably more essential than shelter from life-threatening weather. I wouldn't be shocked if Mrs. Henderson herself was out there, hat and all, personally delivering updates door to door. Her conspiracy theories wait for no storm."

I chuckled at the mental image of Mrs. Henderson battling the elements, her elaborate hat serving as both news delivery system and impromptu sail. But my mirth was short-lived as I remembered the gravity of our situation. "As much as I'd love to properly appreciate our paperboy's dedication to journalism in the face of potential death by flying debris, we've got work to do. Let's have a quick breakfast and then head out to continue our investigation. The egg's not going to find itself."

I popped some bread in the toaster for myself and dished out the promised premium cat food for Ginger. As he tucked in with gusto, he paused to fix me with a stern look, a bit of gourmet fish dangling comically from his whiskers.

"Just so we're clear," he said between bites, "this is a one-time thing. Don't expect to bribe your way out of our morning runs every day. I won't always be susceptible to gastronomic persuasion."

"Wouldn't dream of it," I assured him, though I couldn't quite keep the hopeful note out of my voice. "I'm sure tomorrow I'll be raring to go, wind, rain, or shine."

Breakfast finished, I dialed Aaron's number, the phone cradled between my ear and shoulder as I rinsed our dishes.

He picked up on the third ring, his voice still gravelly with sleep.

"Morning, Aaron," I said, trying to inject some cheer into my voice. "Are you and Lily up and ready to head out for some investigative work? The game is afoot, as they say."

There was a pause, then a muffled yawn. "We're up, yeah. But heading out? In this weather? Is that safe? I'm pretty sure I just saw Mary Poppins float by on her umbrella."

In the background, I could hear Lily's excited voice, a stark contrast to her father's sleepy concern. "Is that Mr. Butterfield? Tell him I'm ready for the next steps in the investigation!"

"No need to relay that," I said quickly, unable to suppress a smile at Lily's enthusiasm. "I heard her loud and clear. Look, we'll all pile into my car and drive to the office. We need to dig up some information on those engineers from Victor's company and see if we can contact them. Maybe we'll solve this case before the storm blows us all to Oz."

Aaron sighed, a sound of resignation that spoke volumes about the trials of parenting an enthusiastic young detective-in-training. "I guess there's no stopping Hurricane Lily when she gets like this. Alright, we'll meet you outside in ten minutes. I'll bring life jackets, just in case."

***

The drive to the office was an adventure in itself. The wind buffeted the car, sending it swaying alarmingly at times. I gripped the steering wheel so tightly my knuckles turned white, silently praying to whatever deity might be listening that we'd make it in one piece.

From the backseat, Lily piped up, her face illuminated by the glow of her phone. She seemed entirely unperturbed by our vehicular acrobatics. "Did you know that the fastest wind speed ever recorded was 253 miles per hour? That's like, super fast! Don't worry though, this storm won't get nearly that bad. According to the weather app, it should actually calm down by this afternoon."

"Thank heavens for that," Ginger muttered from his perch on Lily's lap. "I was beginning to think Jim's ancient chariot might actually transform into a flying machine. Though given its usual performance, I'm not sure it would fare any better in the air. We'd probably end up being the first cat and human team to accidentally circumnavigate the globe."

We made it to the office in one piece, though I was certain I'd aged a few years in the process. As we filed inside, shaking off the rain like a group of bedraggled dogs, Aaron glanced around, taking in the cluttered but cozy space.

"Hasn't changed much since my last visit," he observed, running a hand along a shelf lined with case files and dusty knick-knacks. "Though there seem to be more notes and papers now."

I shrugged, moving toward my desk and nearly tripping over a stack of old newspapers I'd been meaning to recycle. "Cases don't solve themselves. Got to keep track of everything. You never know when a seemingly insignificant detail might crack a case wide open."

"Yes," Ginger chimed in, leaping gracefully onto the desk and narrowly avoiding knocking over a precariously balanced mug of pens, "especially the intricate details of Mr. Whiskers' preferred hiding spots. Vital information, that. You never know when the location of a grumpy cat might solve a century-old mystery."

I gestured for Aaron and Lily to take a seat as I fired up my trusty old laptop. The machine wheezed to life with a sound not unlike an asthmatic dragon. Lily's eyes widened as she took in the dated machine, her expression a mix of fascination and disbelief.

"Wow, I've never seen a computer that old before," she said, leaning in for a closer look. "What year is it from?"

Aaron chuckled. "Probably before you were born, honey. I think I had a similar model when I was in college. It was cutting edge back then."

I patted the laptop affectionately. "It may be old, but it's reliable. They don't make them like this anymore. Built to last, unlike these newfangled gadgets that need replacing every other week."

No sooner had the words left my mouth than the screen flickered and died, replaced by the dreaded blue screen of death. The irony was not lost on me, nor on Ginger, who let out a snort of amusement.

"You were saying?" he drawled, his tail swishing with undisguised glee. "I see your 'built to last' model has decided to take an unscheduled coffee break. Shall we wait for it to finish its existential crisis, or should we consider upgrading to something from this century?"

Muttering under my breath, I gave the laptop a gentle pat, as if that might coax it back to life. "Come on, old friend. Don't fail me now. We've got a case to solve."

Lily leaned forward, shaking her head with the confidence of a tech-savvy teenager faced with an adult's technological ineptitude. "Oh no, don't do that. Hitting it won't help. Here, let me try something."

Before I could protest, her fingers were flying over the keyboard, tapping out a sequence of commands that looked like gibberish to me. It was as if she was speaking a secret language, communing with the machine in ways I could never hope to understand.

To my amazement, the screen flickered back to life, booting up as if nothing had happened. The desktop appeared, looking smug in its resurrection.

"There you go," Lily said, sitting back with a satisfied smile. "Just a little hiccup. It should be fine now."

I stared at her in awe, feeling every bit my age. "You're a magician. A tech wizard. How did you do that?"

Lily shrugged. "It's no big deal. Just a few tricks I picked up. Computers aren't that complicated once you understand how they think."

"Speak for yourself," I muttered, still marveling at her casual display of technological prowess.

With the computer crisis averted, I settled in to start our search. I began typing in the names of the engineers, my fingers moving with painful slowness over the keys. Each keystroke was a deliberate act, as if I was afraid pressing too hard might cause the entire system to collapse.

After what felt like an eternity, during which I was certain I could hear Ginger's tail swishing in time with my typing, Aaron cleared his throat. "Um, Jim? Maybe it would be faster if Lily did the typing? No offense, but at this rate, the egg might hatch and solve the case for us before you finish typing the names."

I looked up to see Lily practically bouncing in her seat with eagerness, her fingers twitching as if they were magnetically drawn to the keyboard. Swallowing my pride, I nodded and relinquished my seat.

"Go ahead," I said, trying to mask my wounded dignity with a self-deprecating chuckle. "You young folks are better at this sort of thing anyway. At the rate I type, the thief will have sold the egg, retired to a tropical island, and written their memoirs before we find anything useful."

Ginger snickered, his whiskers twitching with barely contained mirth. "I see your technological improvements don't extend to typing speed. Though I suppose we should be grateful you've mastered the art of turning the computer on. Baby steps, as they say."

Lily's fingers flew over the keyboard, bringing up search results faster than I could blink. She clicked through tabs rapidly, scanning and dismissing information at a dizzying pace. It was like watching a hummingbird flit from flower to flower, each movement precise and purposeful.

"Whoa, whoa," I said, feeling slightly overwhelmed and more than a little dizzy. "Could you slow down a bit? I can barely read a sentence before you're onto the next page. My eyes aren't quite as quick as they used to be."

Aaron nodded in agreement, looking equally bewildered. "Even I'm having trouble keeping up, sweetie. And I thought I was pretty good with computers."

Lily looked sheepish, her cheeks flushing slightly. "Sorry, I'm just used to this speed of scrolling. I'll try to slow down. It's just, there's so much information out there, and I wanted to find what we needed faster."

"TikTok generation," Ginger muttered, his tail curling around his paws. "Where attention spans are measured in milliseconds and information is consumed faster than one of Shawn's cocktails on a busy night."

We continued our search, with Lily navigating the digital landscape with impressive skill. After hitting several dead ends, she suddenly let out an excited gasp.

"I think I found something!" she exclaimed, pointing at the screen. "It's an archived webpage from NautiluxTech Innovations – their employee page."

We all leaned in closer. There, listed among other names, were Aiden Wright and Ethan Zhao. Both appeared to be young men in their twenties. Ethan had Asian features, his dark eyes holding a spark of intelligence. Aiden, on the other hand, was white with a neatly trimmed beard and buzz cut. Something about Aiden's eyes tugged at my memory, though I couldn't pinpoint exactly why.

"Is there any contact information?" I asked hopefully, squinting at the screen.

Lily shook her head. "Just their names and positions. No phone numbers or email addresses."

"Alright," I said, thinking quickly. "Let's try searching for them individually. Start with Aiden Wright – he seems familiar. Maybe we can find some social media profiles."

Lily's fingers danced across the keyboard once more, bringing up search after search. But our hunt for Aiden turned up nothing. It was as if the man had vanished into thin air, leaving no digital footprint behind.

"He's like a ghost," Aaron commented, frowning. "In this day and age, it's strange for someone to have no online presence at all."

"Maybe he's a secret agent!" Lily suggested, her eyes lighting up at the possibility.

"Let's not jump to conclusions just yet. Okay, let's try Ethan Zhao then," I suggested.

This time, we struck gold. Lily found a news article from two years ago, featuring a photo of a slightly older Ethan.

The headline proclaimed him a hero for saving a man who had fallen overboard during a storm at sea.

"So he went from engineer to sailor and hero," Aaron mused. "That's quite a career change."

But my mind was racing down a different path. Ethan had become a sailor after his engineering career? Could he possibly be on that mysterious ship Robert had spotted on his radar?

Chapter 10

"This sounds like another piece of a puzzle," I said, leaning back in my chair and rubbing my chin thoughtfully. "A mysterious ship appears in these waters on the day of the theft, and the engineer who sold the drone which was used in the theft became a sailor. So, he could be on that ship."

Lily's eyes lit up at that idea, her excitement palpable in the small, cluttered office. The glow from the computer screen highlighted the eager spark in her gaze. "That would make sense!" she exclaimed, her words tumbling out in a rush. "And that means he could have an accomplice on land to make the theft possible. It's like something out of a spy movie!"

Aaron, ever the voice of reason, held up a hand to temper his daughter's enthusiasm. "Let's not get ahead of ourselves so quickly," he cautioned. "We don't even know if that ship is real, or if it was just Robert's radar malfunctioning. We should wait for news from Robert about that ship before jumping to conclusions."

Ginger, who had been lounging on a stack of old case files, lifted his head and fixed me with a look that practically oozed skepticism. "I hate to admit it, but the voice of reason has a point," he meowed. "Even if that ship is real, Ethan being on it could be such a coincidence worthy of a Hollywood spy thriller. There are thousands of ships on this planet. Why would he be on that exact ship, given that the ship is real, of course? It's about as likely as you suddenly developing a talent for technology."

"It's just a theory," I conceded, absently shuffling some papers on my desk. The familiar rustling sound was oddly soothing. "But if there's one thing I've learned from our previous cases, it's that we shouldn't eliminate any possibility, even if it seems like a convenient coincidence. Remember the Christmas case? Who would have thought a bookstore owner would be behind all that?"

The sudden shrill ring of my phone cut through the contemplative atmosphere, making us all jump. I fumbled for a moment, nearly knocking over a precariously balanced stack of files, before managing to extract the device out of my pocket. The screen displayed an unknown number.

"Hello?" I answered, curiosity coloring my tone.

"Mr. Butterfield?" Dorothy's familiar voice came through, tinged with a hint of anxiety. "It's Dorothy Collins from the museum."

"Dorothy, hello," I replied, quickly putting the phone on speaker so everyone could hear. "Is everything alright?

Did you remember something or learn something important?"

There was a slight pause, filled only by the faint static of the phone line. When Dorothy spoke again, her voice was heavy with worry. "Not yet, I'm afraid. I'm just calling to ask how the investigation is going. I'm so nervous that such a precious artifact was stolen on my watch. I can't help but feel responsible."

My heart went out to her. I could practically picture her wringing her hands, her usually impeccable appearance probably showing signs of stress. "It's not your fault, Dorothy," I assured her, my voice gentle but firm. "These things happen, even with the best security measures in place. We have a couple of leads, though they seem a bit far-fetched at the moment."

Dorothy's sigh was audible even through the phone's tinny speaker. "I had hoped you and your friends could make progress faster," she admitted. "Because yesterday when you left, the police seemed busier blaming everyone on the staff for the disappearance of the egg than actually trying to find it. They even blamed those poor students!"

I couldn't help but roll my eyes. "That sounds like our local law enforcement," I muttered. Then, struck by a thought, I added, "Actually, I wanted to ask you a couple of questions about the museum staff, just to clarify a few things. Would that be okay?"

"Of course," Dorothy replied, a hint of relief in her voice. "You can ask me anything."

I paused, considering. While phone conversations were convenient, they lacked the nuance of face-to-face interactions. I couldn't read Dorothy's body language or facial expressions over the phone, and those subtle cues could be crucial. "You know what?" I said, making a quick decision. "I think it might be better if we meet in person. Would that be possible?"

"Oh," Dorothy sounded surprised. "Well, I'm at home right now, but with this storm outside... I worry about how you'd get here safely."

I glanced out the window, where the wind was still howling, though it seemed to have lost some of its earlier fury. "Don't worry about that," I assured her. "My car can endure any kind of weather. What's your address?"

After Dorothy gave me her address, I told her we'd be there in five minutes and ended the call. Turning to the others, I announced, "Change of plans. Ginger and I are going to head over to Dorothy's place to ask some questions. Lily, Aaron, can you two continue searching here? See if you can dig up any more details on Ethan Zhao, maybe even find his contact information."

Lily nodded eagerly, her fingers already poised over the keyboard. "We're on it, Mr. Butterfield! We'll let you know if we find anything important."

Aaron's expression was more serious as he met my gaze. "Be careful out there," he warned. "Not just because of the storm, but with the interviews too. One of the staff could be the thief, and therefore potentially dangerous."

I nodded, appreciating his concern. "We'll be careful," I promised. "Ready, Ginger?"

Ginger stretched lazily. "As ready as I'll ever be to venture out into this charming recreation of Noah's flood," he drawled. "Though I must say, I'm looking forward to seeing how your driving skills hold up against Mother Nature's temper tantrum."

***

The drive to Dorothy's house was less harrowing than I'd anticipated. The wind had indeed died down somewhat, though rain still pelted the windshield with impressive force. As we pulled up to the curb outside a neat, two-story house with pale yellow siding, I felt a sense of relief.

"Well, that wasn't so bad," I commented, putting the car in park. "Looks like Lily was right about the storm calming down."

Ginger, who had spent most of the journey with his eyes squeezed shut and his claws dug into the passenger seat, opened one eye cautiously. "I suppose even the weather occasionally takes pity on your driving abilities," he muttered. "Though I think I've aged several years in cat time during that little adventure."

We hurried up the neatly maintained path to Dorothy's front door. The flowerbeds on either side, though battered by the storm, still showed signs of careful tending. I raised my hand to knock, but before my knuckles could make contact, the door swung open.

Dorothy stood there, looking slightly frazzled but managing a warm smile. "Mr. Butterfield, Ginger, come in quickly," she urged, ushering us inside. "Get out of this dreadful weather."

As we stepped into the entryway, I noticed a small, long-bodied dog peering curiously at us from behind Dorothy's legs. Its floppy ears perked up at the sight of newcomers, and its tail began to wag tentatively.

Dorothy followed my gaze and smiled fondly. "Oh, this is Herbie," she introduced, reaching down to pat the dachshund's head. "He's harmless, really. Loves to play. I hope he and Ginger will be friends."

I glanced down at Ginger, who was eyeing Herbie with a mixture of disdain and resignation. "A dachshund named Herbie?" he meowed quietly. "Let me guess, because he likes eating herbs? A vegan dachshund. That's certainly a new one. What's next, a vegetarian shark?"

Suppressing a smile at Ginger's commentary, I followed Dorothy into her living room. The space was cozy and inviting, with overstuffed armchairs, shelves lined with books, and framed photographs covering nearly every available surface. The air smelled faintly of cinnamon and old books, a comforting combination.

"Please, make yourselves comfortable," Dorothy said, gesturing to the seating options. "Can I get you anything? Coffee? Tea?"

I considered for a moment. I'd already had coffee this morning, and more caffeine might make me jittery. "A cup of herbal tea would be lovely, thank you," I replied.

As Dorothy bustled off to the kitchen, I settled into one of the armchairs. Ginger remained alert on the floor, his tail swishing as he surveyed the room. Herbie, seemingly emboldened by Dorothy's absence, trotted over to investigate the newcomers.

"You know," Ginger muttered, eyeing the approaching dachshund warily, "I see you've learned nothing from the past. Still accepting beverages from potential suspects. Need I remind you how that worked out with Brenda?"

I shook my head, keeping my voice low. "I don't think Dorothy is a suspect," I argued. "She helped us find Lily, remember? And we watched the footage from the entrance – Dorothy was behind the reception desk all morning."

Ginger's whiskers twitched skeptically. "Brenda seemed helpful at first too, and we both know how that turned out. I'm just saying, a little caution wouldn't hurt. Unless you're secretly hoping for another long nap after your tea."

Before I could retort, Herbie reached us. The little dog sniffed curiously at Ginger before, to my great amusement, giving the cat's cheek a friendly lick. Ginger's expression of utter indignation was priceless.

I chuckled. "Looks like you'd better keep your new friend busy while I question Dorothy," I teased. "Who knows? You might find some common ground. Maybe swap stories about chasing squirrels or the best sunny spots for napping."

Ginger's only response was a look of such profound disgust that I had to bite my lip to keep from laughing out loud.

Dorothy returned a few minutes later, carrying a tray with two steaming cups of tea. She smiled warmly when she saw Herbie sitting close to Ginger, his tail wagging happily. "Oh, look at that! They've already become friends. How wonderful!"

"Yes, they seem to be getting along," I agreed, throwing a mischievous glance at Ginger. If looks could kill, I'd have been six feet under.

As Dorothy and I settled in to talk, I couldn't help but notice Ginger's predicament out of the corner of my eye. Herbie, apparently deciding that Ginger was his new best friend, kept trying to engage the cat in play. He'd bring over toys, wag his tail hopefully, and even attempt to initiate games of chase. Ginger, for his part, did his best to maintain his dignity, but I could see his resolve weakening with each passing minute.

"So," Dorothy said, pulling my attention back to the matter at hand, "what was it you wanted to ask me about?"

I took a sip of my tea – a refreshing peppermint, I noted – and set the cup down carefully. "I wanted to talk about your staff," I began. "How long they've been working at the museum, how well you know them – that sort of thing. And I'd like to start with Ben, if that's alright. He's the one I haven't had a chance to interview yet, given his... indisposition during the theft."

Dorothy's face softened at the mention of Ben. "Oh, Ben is a wonderful man," she said warmly. "He's been working at the museum even longer than I have. Did you know he once stayed three hours after closing to help a little boy find his lost teddy bear? Or the time he managed to secure a last-minute donation to save our endangered butterfly exhibit?"

As Dorothy continued to sing Ben's praises, I asked carefully, "But if he's so responsible, how did he end up... out of commission during such a crucial time?"

Dorothy's smile faltered slightly. "Well, after he finally emerged from the restroom, he gave a statement to the police. Apparently, he ate half of a protein bar that some guests had left on a windowsill. Shortly after, he was struck with such severe stomach pains that he had to rush to the bathroom."

I frowned, a familiar sense of unease settling in my stomach. "Another poisoning in our town?" I mused aloud. "It's becoming something of a trend."

Dorothy nodded gravely. "The police took the other half of the bar for testing. We're all hoping it was just a case of food gone bad, but given recent events..."

"Let's hope Dr. Chen and her team can determine what was in that protein bar," I said. "I'll give her a call later to check on the progress." Making a mental note to follow up on that, I moved on to my next question. "What about Max? How long has he been with the museum?"

"I hired Max about two years ago," Dorothy replied. "It was after our previous guard retired. To be honest, it was for the better – the old guard couldn't keep up with the modern security technologies we were implementing."

I nodded, feeling a twinge of sympathy. The situation reminded me all too well of my own firing from the library. Sometimes progress left people behind, no matter how dedicated they were.

Dorothy continued, her tone thoughtful. "To be honest, Max isn't exactly a tech wizard either, but he's still better than his predecessor. He's reliable, and that counts for a lot in this line of work. It's not easy these days to find a security guard who's reliable, strong, and also good with technology. Sometimes you have to prioritize certain qualities."

"And there haven't been any incidents regarding Max's security capabilities?" I probed gently.

Dorothy shook her head. "None at all. Oh, it was a bit rocky at first – he struggled with mastering the security system and cameras. But he improved steadily. He's still not perfect, mind you, but he's come a long way. And he's excellent at spotting suspicious activity among the guests. He and Ben make quite the team."

I leaned forward slightly. "So you trust them both completely?"

"Absolutely," Dorothy said without hesitation, her voice firm. "They're the backbone of our security team."

Nodding thoughtfully, I moved on to my final question. "And what about Josh? What can you tell me about him?"

Dorothy's face lit up. "Oh, Josh is a good guy. Very responsible. He's only been with us for a month, but he's already proven to be quite effective. His cleaning work is impeccable – you should see how he gets those display cases to shine!"

I blinked, my train of thought suddenly derailing. "Wait a minute," I interrupted, holding up a hand. "Did you say he's only been working at the museum for a month?"

Chapter 11

Dorothy nodded, looking slightly perplexed by my reaction. "Yes, that's right. Is that... significant?"

My mind was racing, pieces of the puzzle rearranging themselves in light of this new information. Josh, the newest addition to the staff, had been the one cleaning in the room next to the exhibit when the theft occurred. And now, learning that he'd only been there a month...

"It might be," I said slowly, meeting Dorothy's confused gaze.

As I considered this new information, I heard a commotion behind me. Turning, I saw Ginger looking thoroughly annoyed, with Herbie hot on his heels. The dachshund was carrying a squeaky toy in his mouth, tail wagging furiously as he tried to entice Ginger into a game.

"I don't suppose," Ginger meowed, his dignity clearly hanging by a thread, "that you could wrap this up soon? I'm not sure how much more 'bonding' I can take with my new 'friend' here."

I suppressed a smile, knowing we had to follow this lead. Ginger could endure a bit more of Herbie's enthusiasm.

Turning back to Dorothy, I asked, "Where did Josh work before the museum?"

Dorothy sighed. "He moved to Oceanview Cove looking for a small town life. Apparently, he couldn't find a job in the city. I hired him because he was in desperate need of work, and we were in desperate need of a janitor. Young people nowadays, they all want to be bloggers, influencers. No one wants to do real jobs anymore."

I nodded in agreement. "That's right. Say, could you tell me where Josh lives? I'd like to ask him more about his job-hunting experiences in the city, and maybe a few follow-up questions about yesterday morning."

"Of course," Dorothy replied. "He rents a small apartment on Main Street."

Dorothy then provided the detailed address, which I jotted down in my notepad. I glanced at Ginger, who had finally given in and was now engaged in an undignified game of tug-of-war with Herbie, looking thoroughly disgruntled.

"I think that's all the questions I have for now," I said, rising from my seat. "Thank you for your time, and for the tea. It was delicious."

Dorothy stood as well, her brow furrowed with concern. "Of course, Mr. Butterfield. But... is everything alright? You seemed quite startled by what I said about Josh."

I paused, considering how much to reveal. "It's probably nothing," I said carefully. "Just a detail that caught my attention. We'll look into it."

As we made our way to the door, Herbie trailing behind us with his toy still clutched hopefully in his mouth, Dorothy's worried voice stopped us. "You don't think Josh could have anything to do with the theft, do you? He's such a nice young man."

I turned back to face her, my expression carefully neutral. "We shouldn't eliminate any possibilities at this stage," I said gently. "As I mentioned, I just want to ask Josh a couple of questions. It's all part of the investigation process."

We bid Dorothy farewell and stepped outside. Both the rain and wind had weakened considerably.

As we settled into our seats in the car, Ginger let out a long sigh. "Finally," he meowed. "My patience was wearing thin with that Herbie."

I chuckled. "Oh come on, you two seemed like best friends by the end there."

Ginger fixed me with a withering glare. "If by 'best friends' you mean 'reluctant participants in canine-induced torture', then sure." He paused, his expression turning serious. "So, do you think we've stumbled upon another coincidence? New janitor comes to work at the museum, and in a month a priceless egg gets stolen?"

I shrugged, starting the car. "Let's hear what he has to say first. It could be nothing, or it could be everything. In this town, you never know."

***

As we pulled up to the curb on Main Street, the rain had dwindled to a light drizzle, leaving behind a damp sheen on the pavement. The storm clouds were gradually dispersing, with patches of blue sky beginning to peek through on the horizon.

I killed the engine and turned to Ginger, who was eyeing the nondescript apartment building across the street with his usual air of feline skepticism. "Ready to meet our potential suspect?"

Ginger's tail twitched, his whiskers bristling slightly. "As ready as I'll ever be to potentially confront a criminal mastermind in his lair. Though given our town's track record, he's more likely to trip over his own shoelaces than orchestrate a daring escape."

Chuckling at Ginger's assessment, I stepped out of the car, the cool damp air hitting my face like a refreshing slap. The scent of wet asphalt and blooming spring flowers filled my nostrils as we made our way across the street.

The apartment building was a squat, three-story structure with peeling paint and a slightly crooked front stoop. A rusty buzzer panel stood by the front door, its faded labels barely legible. I ran my finger down the list of names until I found "J. Foster" and pressed the button.

For a long moment, there was only silence, broken by the occasional drip of water from the building's sagging gutters. Then, a crackle of static, followed by a hesitant voice: "Who is it?"

"Josh? It's Jim Butterfield and my partner Ginger," I replied, leaning close to the speaker. "I'd like to ask some follow-up questions regarding the theft, if you don't mind."

The silence that followed was so prolonged that I began to wonder if the intercom had malfunctioned. I was about to press the buzzer again when Josh's voice finally came through, thin and uncertain. "Yes?"

Frowning at the odd response, I pressed on. "Great. Mind if we come up? It's still pretty wet out here."

Another pause, shorter this time, before Josh's voice crackled through once more. "Right, of course."

The door buzzed open, and we stepped into a narrow hallway that smelled faintly of old cigarettes and lemon-scented cleaning products. The worn carpet muffled our footsteps as we made our way to the stairs.

"I do hope our potential criminal mastermind doesn't have any furry accomplices waiting to greet us," Ginger muttered as we climbed. "I've had quite enough of overly enthusiastic four-legged companions for one day."

"Don't worry, partner. I'm sure Josh is more of a fish person. Maybe a nice, quiet goldfish that won't try to engage you in any games."

As we reached the second-floor landing, I spotted Josh standing in an open doorway, his lanky frame silhouetted against the light from his apartment. His fingers drummed nervously against the doorframe as we approached.

"Any progress on the case?" he asked before we'd even reached him.

I kept my expression neutral as I replied, "Not yet. We're just gathering more information to get the full picture. Mind if we come in?"

Josh hesitated for a fraction of a second before stepping aside. "Sure, come on in."

As we entered the small apartment, the first thing that struck me was the state of disarray. Clothes were strewn about, half-packed bags littered the floor, and there was a general air of hasty preparation. The living room was sparsely furnished, with a threadbare couch, a small TV on a rickety stand, and a coffee table covered in scattered papers and empty takeout containers.

"I thought I'd already answered all the questions," Josh said as he closed the door behind us, his tone a mixture of confusion and wariness.

"Just a couple more," I assured him, my eyes still taking in the chaos of the room. "Are you preparing to go somewhere?"

Josh's Adam's apple bobbed as he swallowed hard. "Yeah, I... I need to take a short vacation. You know, after the stress of the egg theft and all. The museum will be closed for now anyway." He forced a smile that didn't quite reach his eyes. "I'm sure the egg will be found by the time I get back."

I raised an eyebrow. "But you've only worked at the museum for a month. Bit soon for a vacation, isn't it?"

Josh's eyes widened slightly. "How did you know that?"

"I spoke with Dorothy earlier," I explained, watching his reaction carefully. "She mentioned how long you'd been working there, but she didn't say anything about you taking a vacation."

Josh's fingers began to fidget with the hem of his shirt. "Oh, right. Well, I haven't told her yet. It was kind of a spontaneous decision. I was planning to let her know later today."

I nodded slowly, recalling what Dorothy had told me about the staff interviews. "Didn't Sheriff Miller tell you and the other staff after the interviews yesterday not to leave town during the investigation?"

Josh's nervousness seemed to ratchet up a notch. "He didn't say that to me. Does... does anyone suspect me of anything?"

I held up a placating hand. "No, it's just standard practice. He told me the same thing when I found Peter's body and technically became a suspect myself."

Josh's eyebrows shot up. "You were a suspect in a murder?"

I waved off his surprise. "Long story. Let's get back to you, shall we?"

As Josh settled uneasily onto the couch, I took a seat in a worn armchair across from him. Ginger leapt up onto the arm of my chair, his green eyes fixed intently on Josh.

"Dorothy mentioned that you had trouble finding a job in the city before moving here," I began. "What's your background? Why couldn't you find work?"

Josh sighed, running a hand through his disheveled hair. "I graduated from college a few years back, spent a long time job hunting. My parents helped me out during that time. Finally landed a position at a financial company, worked there for almost a year on probation. But then the company went bankrupt, and I lost the job before I even had a chance to become full-time."

He shrugged, a defeated gesture. "After that, I tried to find another job in finance, but you know how it goes. No one wants to hire without full-time experience. So, I just... gave up. Decided to move somewhere with a lower cost of living."

I nodded, understanding the struggle. "Quite a career change, though. From finance to janitorial work."

Josh's lips quirked in a humorless smile. "Yeah, well, I did some soul-searching. Decided I wanted a stress-free life. Living in the city, working in finance... it's intense. This?" He gestured around the small apartment. "It's a stark contrast. And honestly? I kind of enjoy it."

"Yes, living here is stress-free," I replied dryly, "except for the occasional murders, poisonings, and thefts."

Josh chuckled, some of the tension leaving his shoulders. "Still less crime than in the city."

I steered the conversation back to the matter at hand. "Let's talk about the theft. You were cleaning in the room next to the Easter Egg exhibit, right? Didn't you hear anything unusual? The spider drone we suspect was used would have made some noise cutting through the glass."

Josh's eyebrows shot up. "Spider drone? Sounds like something out of a cyberpunk movie."

I blinked, not entirely sure what 'cyberpunk' meant. Before I could ask, Josh continued.

"Anyway, I wouldn't have heard anything. When I'm cleaning, I always have my earphones in. Makes the job more enjoyable, you know? I probably wouldn't have noticed if the dinosaurs came to life and started a conga line, let alone a high-tech drone."

I leaned back in my chair, considering his words. "You do realize how this looks, don't you? Especially to the police. The theft occurred at a very specific time when the only security guard on patrol was indisposed, the other guard was in the security room, the curator was at the reception desk, and you were the only staff member in close proximity to the Easter Egg Room."

Josh's face fell, and he nodded slowly. "Yeah, I get how it looks. Though..." He paused, a thoughtful expression crossing his face. "I'm not entirely sure Ben was indisposed the whole time."

That caught my attention. "What do you mean?"

"Well," Josh said, leaning forward, "I saw Ben rush to the bathroom about an hour before we discovered the egg was missing. That's plenty of time to, you know, do your business, commit a theft, and then go back to the bathroom so no one would suspect anything."

I couldn't help but grimace, remembering Mayor Thompson's extended bathroom visit during the Valentine's Day case. "Trust me, it's entirely possible to be stuck in the bathroom for way longer than an hour."

Josh shrugged. "Maybe. But here's the thing – when I went to clean the Modern History Room, I could have sworn I saw a shadow rushing out of the bathroom. Didn't think much of it at the time, but now? Could have been Ben."

"Or one of those students," I suggested.

"Could be," Josh agreed. "The security footage would show the truth, right?"

The security footage. Of course. If we had more time in the security room, we could check other cameras that weren't covered with photographs. Maybe we could have found some clues there.

Just as I was about to voice this thought, my phone buzzed in my pocket. I fished it out, frowning at the unknown number on the screen.

"Hello?" I answered, curiosity coloring my tone.

"Mr. Butterfield?" A familiar voice came through, tinged with nervous energy. "It's Max, from the museum security. You asked me to call if I remembered anything important. Well, I think I have."

Chapter 12

"Go ahead, Max," I said, bracing myself for whatever revelation was coming.

Max's voice crackled through the phone, brimming with excitement. "I remembered something important about the security cameras, and Ben's protein bar, and the timing of everything, and-"

I held the phone away from my ear as Max launched into a rapid-fire, jumbled explanation that seemed to involve every detail of the past 24 hours. His words tumbled over each other like eager puppies, making about as much sense as one of Mrs. Henderson's conspiracy theories.

"Max," I interrupted, massaging my temple with my free hand. "Max, slow down. I can't understand a word you're saying."

"But Mr. Butterfield, it's all connected! The cameras, the bar, the-"

"Max," I said firmly, channeling my best librarian voice. "Take a deep breath. Where are you right now?"

There was a pause, then a deep inhale and exhale. "I'm at Sophie's bakery," Max said, sounding slightly calmer. "With Ben."

That caught me by surprise. "Ben's there too?"

"Yes, we've been brainstorming, trying to piece everything together, and-"

I could sense another deluge of information coming and quickly cut it off at the pass. "Alright, listen. Ginger and I will come to the bakery now. Don't go anywhere, okay? We'll talk about everything in person."

"But Mr. Butterfield, I just remembered about the-"

"In person, Max," I repeated, then ended the call before he could start again.

I turned to Josh, who was looking at me with a mixture of curiosity and concern. "Was that about the theft? Did they find something?"

I nodded, already moving toward the door. "Yes, but it's not clear exactly what. Max and Ben seem to have remembered some details, but I need to hear it in person to make sense of it all."

Josh's eyebrows shot up. "Ben's involved too? Be careful with him. Remember what I said about that shadow leaving the bathroom."

"I'll keep it in mind," I assured him, my hand on the doorknob. "And Josh? Take my advice – don't go on that vacation just yet. Unless you want to waste money on return tickets when Sheriff Miller inevitably calls you in for more questioning."

Josh's face fell slightly. "I don't think he will. I've already told him everything I know."

"Just consider it," I said, stepping out into the hallway. "Better safe than sorry."

As Ginger and I made our way down the creaky stairs, the smell of mildew and old carpet gave way to the fresh scent of rain-washed air drifting in through an open window. Outside, the storm had finally blown itself out, leaving behind puddles that reflected the patchy blue sky like nature's own funhouse mirrors.

"So, what do you think about Josh?" I asked Ginger as we approached the car.

Ginger's tail swished thoughtfully. "There's definitely something off about him. The timing of his vacation plans is suspiciously similar to that punk Owen from the Valentine's case. Though I must say, if he is our thief, his acting skills rival my ability to pretend I enjoy your attempts at cooking."

"You're right," I said, pulling out my phone. "We need to take some precautions."

I dialed Mrs. Henderson's number, and she answered on the first ring, her voice bubbling with excitement. "Mr. Butterfield! Are you calling to fill me in on all the juicy details of the theft? I'm simply dying to know everything!"

"Not quite yet, Mrs. Henderson," I said, trying to keep my voice low. "But your gossip network might be able to help the investigation. I need you to keep an eye on Josh

Foster and report to me if you see him moving through town with bags."

"Josh Foster?" Mrs. Henderson's voice rose sharply. "The janitor from the museum? Is he a suspect?"

"Please keep your voice down," I said quietly. "He could be a suspect, but we don't want to scare him off. Please don't tell anyone."

"Of course, of course," Mrs. Henderson assured me, her tone conspiratorial. "I can keep secrets, Mr. Butterfield. But I'll inform my network about their new assignment right away."

"Thank you for your help," I said, then ended the call.

I stared at my phone, a knot of worry forming in my stomach. "Did I just make a huge mistake?" I wondered aloud.

Ginger, who had already leapt into the passenger seat, fixed me with a look of feline disdain. "Oh, I'm sure it'll be fine. The whole town will probably know Josh is a suspect before you even start the engine. But hey, at least we'll have comprehensive surveillance, right? Who needs professional detectives when you have an army of nosy neighbors armed with binoculars and an unhealthy interest in other people's business?"

I sighed. "Let's hope we make it to the bakery before the entire town descends on Josh's apartment with pitchforks and torches."

***

The drive to Sophie's bakery was mercifully short, though not without its challenges. A stray garbage can, liberated by the storm, made a kamikaze run at the car, forcing me into an evasive maneuver that had Ginger yowling about whiplash and the indignity of being thrown into the footwell.

The warm glow from the bakery's windows was a welcome sight as we pulled up. The bell above the door chimed cheerfully as we entered, the aroma of fresh-baked goods enveloping us like a warm, yeasty hug.

Sophie looked up from behind the counter, a knowing smile on her face. "Jim," she said by way of greeting, "another holiday, another crime in our little town?"

I couldn't help but chuckle, though it came out sounding more like a tired sigh. "Yes, but at least there are no poisonings or murders this time. I'd call that progress."

Sophie raised an eyebrow. "Right, just a priceless historical artifact stolen. No big deal at all. Should we start taking bets on what'll go missing during the next holiday? My money's on the town hall disappearing during the 4th of July celebration."

Alice, wiping down a nearby table, piped up. "Any suspects yet? Maybe we should start checking the seagulls for suspicious bulges?"

I snorted at the mental image of a seagull waddling away with our precious egg. My eyes darted to the far corner of the bakery, where Ben and Max sat hunched over a table, deep in conversation. I couldn't very well say that one of our suspects might be sitting right here in the bakery.

"We have some leads," I said vaguely, gesturing toward Ben and Max. "In fact, I'm here to discuss them with those two gentlemen over there."

Alice nodded, following my gaze. "Can I get you anything while you're here? Perhaps a 'Solve the Case' special? It's a triple shot espresso with a side of intuition-enhancing croissant."

I considered for a moment. My earlier concerns about caffeine jitters seemed laughable now. What I needed was a jolt to my system, something to sharpen my mind for the conversation ahead.

"An Americano will do, thanks," I said. "And a couple of those intuition-enhancing croissants. Oh, and a saucer of cream for Ginger, of course. He needs all the help he can get with his deductive skills."

Ginger shot me a look that could have curdled milk. "I'll have you know my deductive skills are sharper than your wit, old man. Though that's not saying much these days."

As Alice prepared our order, I made my way to Max and Ben's table, Ginger padding silently beside me. The two men looked up as we approached, their expressions a mix of relief and anxiety.

"Mr. Butterfield," Max said, gesturing to the empty chairs. "Thank you for coming so quickly. We've got so much to tell you, it's like trying to stuff an elephant into a matchbox, but we think we've cracked it, or at least part of it, and-"

I held up a hand, cutting off Max's verbal avalanche. "Slow down, Max. Let's start from the beginning, shall we? And this time, please try to keep it coherent."

Max and Ben exchanged glances before Ben cleared his throat. "Well, Max and I decided to meet up here and brainstorm different scenarios, trying to figure out how we could have let the theft happen right under our noses."

Max nodded eagerly. "We also tried to remember any details that might help find the egg. And boy, did we remember some things. It's like our brains were egg-cellent at hiding information!"

I groaned inwardly at the pun but leaned forward, intrigued. "And what conclusion did you come to?"

Just then, Alice approached with our order, setting down my coffee and croissants along with Ginger's cream. The rich aroma of the coffee wafted up, promising a much-needed boost. Ginger eyed the croissants with interest, and I made a mental note to guard them carefully.

"Thanks, Alice," I said, taking a sip of the steaming brew. It was perfect, strong and smooth, with just a hint of bitterness. Much like this case, I mused. "Now, gentlemen, you were saying?"

Ben took a deep breath, his face reddening slightly. "It all started with that protein bar," he began, looking like he'd rather be anywhere else. "I didn't have time for breakfast that morning, so when I saw it sitting on the windowsill in the Local Legends Room, I figured some visitor had left it behind. I was hungry, so I ate half of it."

He paused, clearly uncomfortable. "What happened next... well, let's just say I spent the next two hours in the bathroom with some severe stomach cramps. I'd rather not go into the details, but let's just say it was not a pleasant experience. I think I saw my life flash before my eyes at one point."

I nodded. "I understand. Please, continue. Though perhaps we could skip the more... graphic details."

Max picked up the thread, his words tumbling out like marbles from an overturned jar. "But here's the thing – we got to thinking, how did that protein bar end up on the windowsill in the first place? Josh is meticulous about cleaning. He'd sooner eat his own mop than leave trash lying around. He would have thrown it away during his end-of-day sweep the evening before Easter."

"And there were no visitors before Ben ate the bar," I finished, the pieces starting to click into place. "The students arrived later."

Ben nodded vigorously, nearly upending his coffee cup. "Exactly! So the only person who could have placed that protein bar there..."

"Was the thief," I concluded. "It was a deliberate attempt to incapacitate you. Clever, if a bit cruel."

"Precisely," Max said, his eyes shining with the excitement of discovery. "We think if we could review the footage from the camera in the Local Legends Room, we might be able to see who placed the bar there."

I felt a surge of excitement, tempered by the nagging feeling that we were still missing something crucial. "That's good thinking. I actually wanted to take a closer look at the camera footage myself."

I hesitated for a moment, then decided to share what Josh had told me. "I just spoke with Josh earlier. He mentioned seeing a suspicious shadow leaving the bathroom right before the estimated time of the theft. He thought it might have been you, Ben."

Ben's face turned an interesting shade of red, somewhere between overripe tomato and sunburned lobster. "What? That's ridiculous! I swear on my mother's grave, I was in that bathroom the entire time. That protein bar hit me like a freight train. I couldn't have left if I wanted to!"

"The security footage will prove it," Max added firmly, a protective note in his voice. "Ben wouldn't steal the egg. He's more likely to lay one himself!"

"I'm a security guard, for crying out loud. My job is to protect the artifacts, not steal them," Ben said, his eyebrows furrowing. Then, as if suddenly registering Max's words, he turned to him and added, "Wait, did you just say I would lay an egg?"

I held up my hands, trying to calm the rising tension. "I'm not suspecting anyone. I'm just relaying what Josh told me. That's why we need to examine the security footage in detail. It could be our best lead."

Just as I finished speaking, my phone buzzed in my pocket. I fished it out, seeing Aaron's name on the screen.

"Excuse me," I said to the group, standing up. "I need to take this."

I stepped away from the table, bringing the phone to my ear. "Aaron? What's up?"

His voice came through, tinged with excitement. "Jim, we found it. We've got Ethan Zhao's phone number."

Chapter 13

"That's great news, Aaron," I said, feeling a spark of excitement ignite in my chest. Finally, we had a solid lead – Ethan Zhao's phone number. "This could help us solve at least one mystery. Have you called the number yet?"

"No," Aaron replied. "We thought it would be better if you made the call. You have more experience with these kinds of negotiations."

I nodded, even though Aaron couldn't see me. "Good thinking. Listen, why don't you and Lily come down to Sophie's Sweet & Savory bakery? We can share information and try calling Ethan together."

"Sophie's bakery?" Aaron repeated. "Is that far from the office?"

"Not at all," I assured him. "It's about a five-minute walk. And the rain has stopped, so it should be a pleasant stroll. Just follow your nose – the smell of fresh pastries will guide you better than any GPS."

Aaron chuckled. "Alright, you've convinced me. We'll be there soon."

"Great, we'll be waiting for you," I said. "Oh, and could you lock up the office before you leave? The key is in the door." I ended the call after Aaron's confirmation.

I made my way back to the table where Max and Ben were waiting expectantly, their faces a mix of curiosity and impatience. The rich aroma of coffee and freshly baked goods enveloped me as I settled back into my seat.

"Good news?" Max asked, leaning forward eagerly. His fingers drummed a rapid, rhythmic pattern on the table's worn surface.

I nodded, feeling a small smile tug at the corners of my mouth. "Could be. Aaron and Lily have managed to track down a phone number for someone who might be able to tell us more about those drones. They're on their way here now."

Max's eyes lit up with renewed hope. "That's great! Maybe we can finally get some answers about those drones. But..." his excitement dimmed slightly, "what about the security footage we were talking about earlier? That could be crucial too."

I set my cup down, the ceramic clinking softly against the saucer. "You're right, Max. We can't overlook that. Where else do you have cameras in the museum? And what else might we be able to learn from the footage?"

Max's face scrunched up in concentration, his eyes taking on a distant look as he mentally mapped out the museum's security system. "Well, we've got cameras in basically every exhibition room. The police checked them, and there were no photographs covering those cameras, so we should be able to see the recordings from all of them."

Ben nodded enthusiastically. "Right, and there's also a camera in the room that precedes the bathroom. We could see who came in and out of there, and it'll prove that I was in there the whole time, just like I said."

I leaned back in my chair, considering their words. The security footage could indeed be a goldmine of information, potentially showing us the thief's movements throughout the museum. But there was one significant obstacle.

"That would be great," I said slowly, "but first we'd have to get access to the security room. And with the museum sealed as a crime scene..."

Max's face fell, his earlier excitement evaporating like morning mist. "You're right. Sheriff Miller shut us out of the security room yesterday, claiming it's part of the police investigation now. We couldn't get another look at the footage. I doubt he'd let anyone in now."

Ben's eyes suddenly lit up, a mischievous glint appearing that reminded me unsettlingly of Lily when she was about to suggest something outrageous. "We could break in through the emergency exit," he said in a stage whisper, leaning across the table conspiratorially. "We've got the keys, after all."

I held up a hand, shaking my head firmly. "No one's breaking in anywhere," I said. "We're not going to solve one crime by committing another. Besides, with our luck, we'd probably trip over Miller taking a nap in there."

Ginger, who had been quietly lapping at his cream, looked up at me with what I could swear was approval in his green eyes. "Finally learning from our mistakes before making reckless decisions," he meowed softly. "I was beginning to worry your penchant for ill-advised plans was a permanent condition. Though I must admit, the image of you tripping over a sleeping Miller is rather amusing."

Suppressing a chuckle, I continued, "I have a friend in law enforcement. I'm sure she can convince Miller to give us access to the security room. It helps the case, after all."

I pulled out my phone, scrolling through my contacts until I found Dr. Chen's number. As I pressed the call button, I silently hoped she'd be willing to help us once again, just as she had when she convinced Miller to give me access to the firearms database.

Dr. Chen picked up on the second ring, her crisp voice coming through clearly. "Mr. Butterfield, what a coincidence. I was just about to call you with some news."

I blinked in surprise, my planned request momentarily forgotten. "Oh? What kind of news?"

"It's about that protein bar one of the guards, Ben, consumed before his... lengthy bathroom occupation," Dr. Chen said, her professional tone tinged with a hint of amusement. "We've analyzed it, and it contains traces of laxative."

I felt a surge of vindication. "I knew it," I said, perhaps a bit too enthusiastically. "The thief must have put it there."

"That seems likely," Dr. Chen agreed. "But it's still unclear how they managed it, especially if the protein bar was sealed. Do you think you could ask Ben about that?"

I glanced at Ben, who was watching me curiously. "Actually, Ben's here with me. Would you mind if I put you on speaker?"

After getting Dr. Chen's agreement, I set the phone on the table and quickly explained the situation to Ben.

"The protein bar was definitely sealed," Ben said. "I distinctly remember that. I wouldn't have eaten an open bar, even if I was starving."

Dr. Chen hummed thoughtfully. "Then it's quite the mystery how the laxative was introduced."

Ben's face had turned an alarming shade of red. "Laxative?" he sputtered. "I swear, when we catch this thief, I'll... I'll..."

"Maybe the thief opened the bar, put the laxative inside, and then resealed it," I suggested quickly, hoping to redirect Ben's anger into something more productive. "With super glue or something similar."

"Good thinking," Dr. Chen said. "I'll examine the wrapper more closely. Now, was there something you wanted to ask me, Mr. Butterfield?"

"Yes, there is," I said. "We need to examine the security camera footage from the museum. It could answer a lot of questions about this case. Do you think you could convince Miller to give us access to the security room? You were able to persuade him about the firearms database before."

Dr. Chen sighed. "I'll try my best, Mr. Butterfield, but I can't promise anything. You know how Miller can be."

"I understand," I replied. "Any help would be crucial at this point."

"Alright, I'll give Miller a call and let you know what he says," Dr. Chen said. "I'll call you back soon."

After ending the call, I looked at Max and Ben. "Well, that's that. Now we wait and hope Miller sees reason."

Max fidgeted in his seat. "Do you really think he'll give us access?"

I shrugged. "Chances are fifty-fifty. But let's hope he does, because I really don't want to resort to... alternative methods."

"But at least it would be more thrilling," Ginger meowed sarcastically. "Nothing says 'Easter fun' quite like some good old breaking and entering. Perhaps we could disguise ourselves as giant rabbits. I'm sure no one would question a six-foot bunny wandering around the museum at night."

Before Ginger could finish his quip, the bell above the bakery door chimed. I looked up to see Aaron and Lily enter, their faces flushed from their brisk walk. The warm, yeasty aroma of fresh-baked goods filled the air, and I saw Lily's eyes widen appreciatively as she took in the display of pastries.

Sophie, ever the attentive host, noticed our new arrivals immediately. "Well, hello there," she called out cheerfully from behind the counter. "New faces in town?"

I stood up, waving Aaron and Lily over. "Sophie, Alice, I'd like you to meet Aaron Robinson and his daughter Lily. They're... old friends, visiting for the Easter Fair."

Sophie's eyes twinkled with interest. "Welcome to Oceanview Cove," she said warmly. "Can I get you anything? We've got some fresh croissants just out of the oven."

Aaron's eyes lit up at the mention of croissants. "Well, after trying Mrs. Abernathy's cookies, I'm inclined to believe that anything baked in this town is going to be delicious."

Sophie beamed with pride. "Especially when they're made by Mrs. Abernathy's star pupil," she said, nodding toward Alice. "Our Alice here has quite the talent for pastry."

Lily's eyes widened. "You can make croissants?" she asked Alice, clearly impressed. "That's so cool! Can you teach me sometime?"

Alice blushed slightly, ducking her head modestly. "I still have a lot to learn," she murmured. "But sure, I'd be happy to show you the basics."

"Nonsense," Sophie said firmly. "You're already perfect. Now, what can I get for you two?"

After placing their orders – an espresso for Aaron, a green tea for Lily, and two croissants with chocolate filling – our newcomers joined us at the table.

Aaron fished out a set of keys from his pocket and handed them to me. "I barely managed to close the office door. You should probably think about changing the locks, Jim."

I accepted the keys with a rueful smile. "I know, I know. I just can't seem to find the time with all these cases."

Ginger looked up from his cream, his whiskers twitching with amusement. "Yes, so many cases. Since the boat racing tournament, we've spent a month looking for lost cats and garden gnomes. Truly riveting stuff."

Max eyed Lily and Aaron curiously. "Backup arrived, I see," he said. "That's good. We need all the help we can get."

I turned to Lily, my curiosity getting the better of me. "So, how did you manage to find Ethan Zhao's number? It couldn't have been easy."

But before Lily could answer, Ben cut in. "Hold on, who's Ethan Zhao? Is he some kind of tech wizard? Or maybe a secret agent?"

I recounted what we learned about Ethan and Aiden, their connection to Victor Sterling's company, and the spider drones' involvement in our case. As I spoke, I could see the pieces clicking into place in Ben's mind. His earlier anger gave way to intense focus, his brow furrowing as he processed this new information.

Lily nodded eagerly when I finished. "Finding Ethan's number was really difficult," she said, her eyes shining with the excitement of the chase. "We searched everywhere online, but there was nothing recent. Then we found his account on this sailors' forum, and there was a comment he'd left under a job ad. He'd put his phone number right there in the comment, saying he was interested in the job. It was like finding a needle in a digital haystack!"

Max leaned forward, nearly knocking over his empty coffee cup in his enthusiasm. "Well, what are we waiting for?" he asked. "Let's call him and get some answers about those drones! Maybe he can tell us how to build our own and we can start a high-tech security business."

Lily pulled a slip of paper from her pocket and handed it to me. I could feel the weight of everyone's expectations as I dialed the number on my phone. The bakery seemed to fall silent around us, the usual chatter and clinking of cups fading into the background as I hit the call button.

"Well," I said, my voice sounding unnaturally loud in the sudden quiet, "here's the moment of truth."

Chapter 14

I held my breath, acutely aware of the weight of everyone's expectations. The warm, yeasty aroma of fresh-baked goods that usually filled me with comfort now seemed cloying and oppressive.

Finally, after what felt like an eternity, there was a click. But instead of Ethan Zhao's voice, a robotic female voice intoned: "The person you are trying to call is unavailable. Please try again later."

I ended the call, unable to hide my disappointment. "No luck," I said, looking up at the expectant faces around the table. "It went straight to voicemail."

Aaron leaned forward, his brow furrowed. "It might just be a connection problem. Try again."

Nodding, I redialed the number. Once again, the robotic voice informed me that the person was unavailable. I tried a third time, and then a fourth, each attempt met with the same frustrating result.

"Are you sure this is the correct number?" I asked, turning to Lily.

She nodded vigorously, her ponytail bouncing with the movement. "Positive. He wrote only this number in his comment on the forum."

Aaron sighed, running a hand through his hair. "His phone is probably off, or maybe there's no signal if he's out at sea."

"Let's hope he sees the missed calls and gets back to us when he has a signal again," I said, trying to inject some optimism into my voice.

Max slumped back in his chair, disappointment etched across his face. "So much for that lead," he grumbled. "I guess we're back to our plan with the security cameras as our best option."

Lily perked up at this, her eyes sparkling with curiosity. "What plan?"

Before I could answer, Alice appeared at our table, balancing a tray laden with Aaron and Lily's order. She set down two steaming cups and a plate of golden, flaky croissants, the rich aroma of chocolate wafting up from their centers.

"Here you go," Alice said with a shy smile. "Two chocolate croissants, an espresso, and a green tea."

"Thank you," Aaron and Lily chorused.

As Alice turned to leave, both father and daughter reached for their croissants simultaneously. They took a bite and let out near-identical sounds of pure enjoyment.

Aaron's eyes widened in surprise. "These are definitely the best croissants I've ever had," he declared, his voice filled with genuine awe.

Lily nodded enthusiastically, a smear of chocolate on her upper lip. "These are wonderful," she told Alice, who was still hovering nearby.

Alice's face flushed at the praise, a pleased smile tugging at her lips. "Thank you," she said softly.

From behind the counter, Sophie beamed proudly. "Told you," she called out. "She's the best."

As Alice retreated, Aaron turned back to me, his expression growing serious once more. "So, what's this plan Max was talking about?"

I took a sip of my now-lukewarm coffee. "We want to get back into the security room at the museum," I explained. "Check the footage from the other cameras in the exhibit rooms. We're hoping it might give us some clues we missed before."

Aaron nodded thoughtfully. "Right, that would clarify a lot of things. It's a shame we didn't have more time to check the footage yesterday before Miller and his team arrived."

"Exactly," I agreed. "So now we're waiting for Dr. Chen to call back and let us know if Miller will give us access to the security room."

As if on cue, my phone began to ring. The shrill sound cut through the bakery's cozy atmosphere, making us all jump slightly.

Ben leaned forward eagerly. "Is that Dr. Chen?"

"Or Ethan?" Aaron chimed in.

Ginger, who had been quietly observing our conversation, chose this moment to add his two cents. "Or maybe it's the Pope himself, calling to congratulate us on Easter?" he meowed sarcastically. "I hear he's quite invested in small-town egg thefts these days."

I glanced at the screen, a small smile tugging at my lips despite the tension. "No, it's just Robert," I said, hitting the answer button and bringing the phone to my ear.

"Jim," Robert's voice came through, tinged with excitement. "I asked around the docks about that ship like you wanted."

I blinked, momentarily confused. "Did I?" Then, the memory clicked into place. "Oh, right. Sorry, with all this information, it slipped my mind. What did you learn?"

Robert chuckled. "Well, one of the fishermen was out at sea just before the full storm hit. He managed to make contact with the ship. Turns out, it's just a fishing vessel."

"A fishing vessel?" I repeated.

"Yep," Robert confirmed. "Because of the storm, they're heading to our harbor. It's the closest one, you see. They need to refuel and make some minor repairs."

I leaned forward, suddenly very interested. "When do you think they'll arrive?"

There was a pause as Robert seemed to be doing some mental calculations. "Well, they said they'd start moving once the storm calmed down. And it's almost settled now, so… I'd say early tomorrow morning. But that depends on their speed, weather conditions, that sort of thing."

"Does this happen often?" I asked. "Fishing ships docking here for refueling and repairs?"

Another pause. "It's happened a couple of times," Robert said slowly. "Usually after severe weather. Not a regular occurrence, mind you, but not unheard of either."

"I see," I replied. "Thanks for the information, Robert. Could you let me know when the ship docks?"

"Sure thing," Robert agreed readily. Then, curiosity crept into his voice. "You expecting someone to be on that ship, Jim?"

"It's possible," I said. "But it's all a bit complicated."

Robert's laugh rumbled through the phone. "As every big case in this town seems to be."

I couldn't help but sigh. "You've got that right."

"Alright then," Robert said, his tone growing brisk. "I'll ask the guys at the docks to keep an eye out for the ship. I'll give you a call when it arrives. Got to go now."

As I ended the call, I found myself the center of attention once more. Aaron leaned forward, his eyebrows raised questioningly. "What did Robert have to say?"

I quickly relayed Robert's information about the approaching fishing vessel. As I finished, a thought struck me. I turned to Lily, who was listening intently while nibbling on her croissant.

"Lily," I said, "what exactly was that job ad for? The one where Ethan left his phone number?"

Lily's eyes widened as realization dawned. "It was for recruiting sailors on a fishing ship!"

The implications of this hit me like a tidal wave. "So the idea of Ethan Zhao being on that fishing ship sailing toward our harbor isn't too far-fetched after all."

Lily turned to Aaron, her expression triumphant. "Dad, you have to admit it's possible now."

Aaron held up his hands in surrender. "Yes, I'll concede that it could be a possibility."

Max, who had been uncharacteristically quiet, suddenly spoke up. "Are you saying that Ethan could actually be more involved in the theft than just being the one who helped create the drone?"

I nodded slowly, the pieces starting to fit together in my mind. "It's looking that way. One of our theories is that Ethan had an accomplice who actually stole the egg."

Ben's eyes lit up with sudden understanding. "And now Ethan's sailing toward the harbor to pick up both his accomplice and the egg!"

I blinked, surprised by Ben's quick deduction. It wasn't an angle I'd considered. "It could be," I admitted.

"The question is," Ginger meowed, "how did Ethan's accomplice get that fancy spider drone? Did Ethan reproduce it all by himself? Because if he did, I might need to reconsider my stance on the intelligence of the human species. Present company excluded, of course."

As I contemplated this new line of questioning, my phone rang again. Before anyone could ask who was calling, I glanced at the screen and announced, "It's Dr. Chen."

I quickly answered and put the call on speaker, saving myself the trouble of relaying the conversation later.

"Mr. Butterfield," Dr. Chen's crisp voice filled the air. "I have two pieces of news for you – one good, one bad. Which would you like to hear first?"

I exchanged glances with the others around the table. "Let's start with the good news," I decided.

"Alright," Dr. Chen said. "I examined the protein bar wrapper as you suggested. There were indeed traces of super glue used to reseal it. Your theory was correct – the thief likely opened the bar, injected the laxative, and then resealed it."

"Great," I said. "At least that's one mystery solved. What's the bad news?"

Dr. Chen's sigh came through clearly. "Unfortunately, Miller refused to grant access to the security footage. I tried to persuade him, but he was adamant. He insists that the police need to study it first, and that no one is to enter or leave the museum."

My heart sank at her words. "Did he give any reason?"

"He claims it's standard procedure," Dr. Chen replied, her tone suggesting she didn't quite believe it. "But between you and me, I think he just wants to solve the case himself for once. Oh, and I overheard him ordering Jones to help Martinez guard the museum. He's doubling the security there."

I ran a hand through my hair, frustration bubbling up inside me. "Thank you for trying, Dr. Chen. We appreciate the effort."

"I'm sorry I couldn't be of more help," she said, genuine regret in her voice.

"Don't worry about it," I assured her. "We'll figure out another way to solve this case."

As I ended the call, a heavy silence fell over our group. Ben was the first to break it, his voice tinged with resignation. "I knew Miller wouldn't let us in."

Max leaned forward, his eyes bright with determination. "So what other ways do we have to solve this case?"

I took a deep breath, my mind racing through our options. Finally, I came to a decision that I knew I might regret later. "We're sticking to our initial plan," I announced. "Forget what I said earlier about avoiding illegal activities. We're breaking in tonight."

Lily's eyes lit up with excitement. "Are we breaking into the museum?" she asked, her voice rising with enthusiasm.

"Shh," I cautioned, glancing around nervously. "Not so loud, please. We don't want the whole town to know." I gave her a concerned look. "And I'm afraid you can't be involved in this, Lily. It could be dangerous."

Lily's face fell for a moment, but then she shook her head firmly. "No way. I'm good with computers. I can help check the footage." She turned to Max, seeking support. "Right?"

Max nodded eagerly. "She's right. We could use her help."

"And I've always wanted to visit a museum at night," Lily added, her eyes sparkling. "Just like in my favorite movie, 'Night at the Museum'!"

"Oh yes," Ginger meowed sarcastically, "because nothing says 'covert operation' quite like a teenage girl living out her Hollywood fantasies. Perhaps we should call up Ben Stiller for some pointers on proper museum etiquette after hours."

I shook my head at Ginger's quip, acknowledging the grain of truth in his words. Turning back to the group, I tried to inject some reason into the conversation. "Look, Martinez and Jones aren't exactly known for their stellar reputations as guards," I admitted. "They're more likely to get spooked by the dinosaur bones than catch any intruders. So our little night expedition might end up resembling that movie more than we'd expect."

Aaron, who had been quietly observing until now, spoke up. "If this is the only way to check the footage, and the guards aren't that competent, then… okay." He fixed me with a stern look. "But I'm not letting Lily go alone. I'm coming too."

I suppressed a groan, realizing our 'little covert operation' was rapidly growing in size. "Alright," I conceded, then turned to Ben. "You said you have keys to the emergency exits, right?"

Ben nodded, patting his pocket. "Right here. We can use them to get in."

"Good," I said. "But we still need a decoy. Someone to keep the guards busy while we slip in." A plan began to form in my mind. "And I think I know just the person for the job."

Ginger, seeming to read my thoughts, let out a soft chuckle. "Oh, I'm sure Jones and Martinez will thoroughly enjoy an impromptu astrology lecture," he meowed. "Nothing says 'riveting night shift' quite like learning about Jupiter's influence on nocturnal vigilance."

Lily, who had been listening intently, suddenly piped up. "Why does this all sound like it's not the first time you've broken in somewhere, Mr. Butterfield?"

I exchanged a glance with Ginger, memories of our past 'adventures' flashing through my mind. "Well," I said slowly, choosing my words carefully, "let's just say Ginger and I... we sometimes implement unorthodox methods in our investigations."

Chapter 15

The night air carried a chill that seemed to seep into my bones as we huddled around the corner from the museum, peering at the darkened building like a group of overgrown children plotting a raid on the cookie jar. Streetlights cast pools of yellow light at regular intervals, barely penetrating the inky darkness between.

My eyes swept over our motley crew – Aaron and Lily, their faces a mix of excitement and apprehension; Max and Ben, looking decidedly nervous but determined; Emma, practically vibrating with barely contained enthusiasm; and of course, Ginger, his tail swishing lazily as he surveyed the scene with his usual feline disdain.

"If it was daytime," I muttered under my breath, "Mrs. Henderson's gossip network would have already figured out we're up to no good."

Ginger's ears twitched. "Bold of you to assume they're not watching us even now," he meowed softly. "I wouldn't put it past that woman to have night-vision goggles and a team of nocturnal spies on retainer. Probably trains carrier pigeons for midnight message delivery too."

I suppressed a chuckle, my eyes scanning the darkened windows of the surrounding buildings. The idea wasn't as far-fetched as it should have been. In Oceanview Cove, you never knew who might be watching.

Leaning in close, I whispered to the group, "Everyone remember the plan?"

A chorus of eager nods greeted me, though I noticed the worry etched into most of their faces. All except Emma, that is. She looked as relaxed as if we were about to embark on a casual stroll through the park.

"I was born for this," she whispered, her eyes twinkling with excitement. The crystals around her neck clinked softly as she shifted.

I raised an eyebrow. "And Plan B? Everyone clear on what to do if things go sideways?"

Aaron's face tightened. "Jim, let's just get this done quickly so we won't have to use Plan B."

I nodded, silently agreeing. Plan B wasn't something I was particularly looking forward to. "Alright then, let's get started with Plan A."

"What, no Plan C?" Ginger quipped. "I'm disappointed, Jim. I thought you were more thorough than that. Should we perhaps devise a Plan D through Z, just to cover all our bases?"

I rolled my eyes. If we needed a Plan C, we'd probably all end up in jail anyway.

Emma, unable to contain herself any longer, began inching toward the guards. "Let's create a distraction," she whispered, her eyes gleaming with mischief.

Before I could give her some final advice, she was off, strolling down the sidewalk as if out for a casual evening walk. I watched, equal parts amused and horrified, as she approached Martinez and Jones, her head tilted back as if studying the night sky.

"Oh!" she exclaimed loudly, colliding with Martinez in a flurry of jangling crystals and fluttering scarves. "I'm so sorry! I was just so caught up in the celestial beauty above us. Did you know that Jupiter is particularly bright tonight? It's in perfect alignment with Venus, which suggests a time of great revelation and discovery!"

Martinez and Jones exchanged bewildered glances, clearly at a loss for how to handle this sudden influx of astrological information. Martinez's hand hovered uncertainly near his belt, as if debating whether to reach for his radio or his notepad.

"Ms. Estrella," Martinez began, trying to inject some authority into his voice, "this is a crime scene and you're not supposed to-"

"Oh, but don't you see?" Emma interrupted, her voice rising with excitement. She gestured wildly, nearly knocking Jones's hat off in the process. "I can help you guard it! The stars have aligned perfectly for increased vigilance and protection. Here, let me show you!"

With a flourish, she produced a handful of crystals from her pocket and began arranging them on the ground in a complex pattern. Jones looked on, his expression a mix of confusion and resignation.

"Well," he said slowly, "I guess a little celestial protection couldn't hurt."

I had to bite my lip to keep from laughing out loud. Emma's performance was Oscar-worthy, and the guards were eating it up.

"Time to move," I whispered to the others. "Let's head for the emergency exit."

We crept along the side of the building, sticking close to the shadows. The sound of Emma's enthusiastic lecture on planetary influences faded as we moved further away. Just as we were nearing the emergency exit, a loud crunch shattered the silence.

Ben froze, his foot hovering over a crushed soda can. The noise seemed to echo in the quiet night air, and a nearby cat startled, dashing away into the shadows.

"Coward," Ginger muttered under his breath.

"What was that?" Martinez's voice carried clearly from the front of the building.

My heart leapt into my throat, but Emma's voice quickly rose, drowning out any response from Jones. "Oh, that must be some cats! Now, where were we? Ah yes, the influence of Mars on nocturnal activities..."

"Be careful," Max hissed at Ben. "You'll get us caught before we even get inside."

Ben mumbled an apology, his face burning with embarrassment in the moonlight. "Sorry," he whispered. "I'm trying."

Finally, we reached the emergency exit. Ben fumbled with his keys for a moment, the metal jingling softly in the night air. After what felt like an eternity, he managed to unlock the door. We slipped inside, enveloped by the musty darkness of the museum's interior.

"I suppose no one thought to bring flashlights," Ginger meowed sarcastically. "How terribly unprepared of us. I bet even the mummies packed better for their eternal rest."

I relayed Ginger's comment to the group, minus the sarcasm. "Did anyone bring a flashlight?"

"Why would we need those?" Lily piped up. "Every phone has a built-in flashlight."

As if to demonstrate, she pulled out her phone and quickly activated its light. Aaron, Max, and even Ben followed suit, filling the hallway with a soft glow.

I stared at my own phone, frantically tapping at icons in an attempt to find the elusive flashlight. The others waited, their impatience almost palpable in the dim light. I could feel Ginger's judgmental stare boring into me.

"Um, Lily?" I finally admitted defeat. "Could you help me turn mine on? Before I accidentally activate one of Emma's meditation apps and fill the museum with the sound of aligning chakras."

Lily bit back a giggle as she took my phone. With a few quick taps, my screen lit up, adding to the pool of light around us. "There you go, Mr. Butterfield."

"Thanks," I mumbled, acutely aware of the generational tech gap. "Alright, let's get to work."

We began making our way through the darkened museum, our phone lights casting eerie shadows that danced across the exhibits. But what should have been a straightforward trek to the security room quickly turned into an impromptu tour, courtesy of our youngest member.

"Oh wow, look at that!" Lily exclaimed, darting over to a display case. Her breath fogged the glass as she pressed close, eyes wide with wonder. "It's just like in 'Night at the Museum'! Do you think these exhibits come to life at night too?"

"Lily," I said, trying to keep the exasperation out of my voice, "we're here to check the security footage, not for a museum tour."

But my words fell on deaf ears. Lily was already moving on to the next exhibit. "Dad, look! It's a real Egyptian sarcophagus! I wonder if it's cursed?"

Aaron chuckled, clearly enjoying his daughter's enthusiasm despite the circumstances. "I don't think we need to add 'angry mummy' to our list of problems tonight, sweetheart."

"Though it might liven things up a bit," Ginger quipped. "I'm sure Miller would love trying to arrest a 3000-year-old pharaoh. I can see the headline now: 'Local

Sheriff Attempts to Read Miranda Rights to Mummified Royalty'."

I sighed, realizing we weren't going to make any progress at this rate. "Aaron, could you maybe...?"

He nodded, understanding my unspoken request. "Lily, honey, we need to focus. Remember why we're here?"

Lily's face fell slightly, but she nodded. "Right, sorry. Security room first, museum tour later."

We continued on, though Lily couldn't resist pointing out interesting artifacts as we passed. By the time we finally reached the security room, I felt like I'd gotten a crash course in the museum's entire collection.

"Alright," I said as we filed into the small room, "let's leave the door open. That way we can hear if the guards decide to come inside for a check."

From outside, I could still hear the faint sound of Emma's voice, punctuated occasionally by confused responses from Martinez and Jones. So far, so good.

Max settled into the chair in front of the bank of monitors, his fingers flying over the keyboard as he logged into the system. "What should we check first?"

"Let's see who came out of the bathroom just before the theft," Ben said immediately. "I want to prove it wasn't me that Josh saw."

I shook my head. "We should check who left the protein bar first. We don't know how much time we have."

But Ben was insistent. "No, I need to clear my name first."

Realizing it would be faster to just humor him, I nodded to Max. "Alright, let's check the footage from the room outside the bathroom."

With Lily's help, Max quickly located the right time frame. We all leaned in, watching intently as the grainy black-and-white footage played out on the screen. The tension in the room was palpable.

"There!" Lily pointed excitedly. "Someone's coming out of the bathroom."

As the figure came into clearer view, I felt a mix of relief and confusion. It wasn't Ben, as Josh had suspected, but one of the paleontology students.

"See?" Ben said triumphantly. "I told you it wasn't me!"

"So Josh really did see someone," I mused.

Aaron frowned. "Could the student have placed the protein bar?"

I shook my head. "Unlikely. The students arrived after Ben had already eaten the bar and been... indisposed for quite some time."

"At this point, nothing would surprise me," Max said, shaking his head. "For all we know, that student could have a secret teleportation device."

"Ooh, can we check for that next?" Lily asked eagerly, her eyes lighting up at the possibility.

"Let's focus on what we came for," I said gently, trying to redirect her enthusiasm. "We need to see who placed that protein bar on the windowsill in the Local Legends Room."

Max nodded, pulling up the footage from the correct camera. Lily, proving herself to be quite adept with the system, quickly found the right time frame, starting from the evening before Easter.

"Look," Max commented as the footage played, "there's Josh cleaning the room at the end of his shift. No protein bar on the windowsill then."

We watched as Lily fast-forwarded through the night, the camera switching to night vision mode as the museum grew dark. The black-and-white footage gave everything an otherworldly quality.

"Hold on," Aaron said suddenly. "If the cameras record at night, did they catch us coming in just now?"

Max waved a hand dismissively. "Don't worry, I'll clear all that footage. And I'll set the cameras to stop recording for five minutes when we leave, so we can get out safely."

I blinked in surprise. "Wait, you can do that? Just stop the recording for a specific time?"

"Yeah," Max nodded. "Pretty cool technology, right?"

As Lily continued to scan through the footage, we all leaned in closer, eyes straining for any sign of the protein bar appearing. The room was silent except for the soft hum of the computers and our collective breathing.

Suddenly, Lily let out a frustrated huff. "It's gone!"

"What's gone?" Aaron asked, leaning in even closer.

"The footage," Lily explained, rewinding and playing the section again. "Look, there's a chunk missing. One second the windowsill is empty, and the next..." She paused the video, pointing to the screen. "The protein bar just appears out of thin air."

"I don't believe it," Max breathed. "The thief deleted part of the footage."

I nodded slowly, the pieces starting to come together. "So the thief was definitely in this room. They turned off the alarm and deleted the footage."

A thought struck me. "Max, how many times did you leave the security room yesterday morning?"

Max's face flushed slightly. "Only once, but... for about ten minutes. I had a bit of a bathroom emergency too. Nothing to do with that protein bar though – just had a big breakfast."

"Yeah, I can confirm it," Ben chimed in. "We had a good conversation in there. At least someone kept me company."

Ginger snorted. "Wonderful. Two security guards having a chat in the bathroom instead of, oh I don't know, guarding the priceless artifacts. Stellar work, gentlemen. I'm sure the egg thief sent you a thank you note for making their job so much easier."

I stroked my chin thoughtfully, considering the implications. "So it's entirely possible that the thief used that time to turn off the alarm and clear the footage."

Aaron nodded. "Ten minutes would be more than enough time."

"Is there a camera that points at the security room door?" I asked Max.

He shook his head. "Unfortunately not. Ms. Collins said the museum barely had the budget for cameras in the exhibit rooms. No one thought someone would try to break into the security room itself."

"Of course not," Ginger meowed sarcastically. "Why would anyone want to break into the room that controls all the security systems? Clearly, that's the last place a thief would go. Maybe next time they should just leave the key under a welcome mat."

Before I could ask another question, a familiar tune suddenly filled the air. The gospel rendition of "Stayin' Alive" echoed through the small room, making us all freeze in horror.

"Is there someone inside the museum?" Martinez's voice drifted in from outside, sounding both confused and slightly terrified.

With shaking hands, I reached for my phone. Sarah's name flashed on the screen. Of course it would be her, calling at the worst possible moment. I made a mental note to have a serious talk with my daughter about the concept of "reasonable calling hours."

I quickly dismissed the call, and the silence that followed seemed deafening. We all held our breath, straining to hear if the guards had been alerted to our presence. The only sound was the soft whirring of the computer fans and our own rapid heartbeats.

"Mr. Butterfield," Lily whispered, her voice tight with worry, "what do we do?"

I took a deep breath, trying to project a calm I didn't feel. "You continue searching the other cameras," I said. "Ginger and I will set Plan B in motion."

Chapter 16

As Ginger and I slipped out of the security room, closing the door with a soft click behind us, my heart pounded so loudly I was certain the guards outside would hear it. I took a deep breath, trying to calm my jangling nerves.

This was it – Plan B. The first step was for Ginger and me to draw attention to ourselves and lead the guards as far away from the security room as possible. If we got caught, at least we'd be the only ones taking the fall. With any luck, I could explain it away as overzealous investigating for the case.

Who was I kidding? When had luck ever been on our side in this town?

As if to prove my point, my phone erupted once again in the gospel rendition of "Stayin' Alive." The cheerful disco beat echoed through the quiet museum halls, sounding impossibly loud in the stillness.

"It's that disco ghost phone again!" Jones's voice drifted in from outside, a mix of excitement and fear.

"I thought you were joking about that," Martinez replied, sounding skeptical but unnerved. "But it seems like it might be real after all."

"I never joke about something like that," Jones said solemnly. "We should head in and check it out."

Emma's voice piped up, a last desperate attempt to stop them. "Oh, it's probably nothing! Wouldn't you gentlemen rather hear more celestial predictions? I was just about to explain how Saturn's rings influence police interrogation techniques!"

"Thank you, Ms. Estrella," Martinez said firmly, "but we've got to do our job."

The front door creaked open, the sound unnaturally loud in the quiet museum. Ginger and I ducked into the Agricultural History Room just in time, pressing ourselves against the wall behind a display case showcasing old farming tools. My heart was in my throat, and I could feel Ginger's fur standing on end where he pressed against my leg.

"Is that Sarah calling again?" Ginger asked in a low meow, his whiskers twitching with annoyance.

I nodded, glancing at the still-ringing phone. "Yes."

"Why isn't she asleep? It's nearly midnight – time for sleep, certainly not for ill-timed phone calls. Though I suppose breaking and entering isn't exactly a daytime activity either."

"Maybe she wants to say something important," I whispered back. "I'll call her once we're out of this mess. Assuming we don't end up in jail, that is."

This time, instead of immediately dismissing the call, I let it ring. The guards would follow the sound, hopefully leading them away from the security room.

It worked like a charm – Jones and Martinez entered the Agricultural History Room, their flashlight beams dancing across the exhibits as they followed the persistent disco beat. As soon as they entered, I dismissed the call, praying Sarah wouldn't try again. The abrupt silence was almost as jarring as the ringtone had been.

"It stopped," Martinez said, sounding confused. His flashlight beam swept past our hiding spot, and I held my breath. "Maybe it's not real after all."

"No, it definitely is," Jones insisted, his voice thick with excitement. "We'll find it. Maybe it's hiding behind one of these old plows. Do ghost phones like farming equipment?"

They began to search the room, moving methodically from one display to the next. Ginger and I circled around behind them, using the exhibits as cover. We were almost to the door when my phone started ringing again. The sudden burst of disco music in the quiet room nearly made me jump out of my skin.

Martinez and Jones perked up instantly at the sound. Without thinking, I grabbed Ginger and bolted for the next room, dismissing the call as we ran. I silently hoped that three dismissals would be enough for Sarah to realize I was busy.

"I heard footsteps!" Martinez called out, his voice echoing through the museum. "Does this disco ghost phone have legs?"

"I don't know," Jones replied. "But it could be not a disco ghost phone at all, but an intruder who's playing with us."

"Oh no," Martinez moaned. "That's even scarier. I didn't sign up for ghost hunting or burglar chasing!"

"Don't be scared," Jones said, trying to sound brave. "We'll catch them. How hard can it be to outrun a phone? Even if it is possessed."

The next few minutes unfolded like a scene from a silent film comedy. Ginger and I dashed from room to room, always just one step ahead of the bumbling guards. Jones and Martinez seemed to spook at every exhibit, jumping at shadows and whispering frantically to each other.

As we snuck past the Egyptian exhibit, I heard Martinez hiss, "Do you think that mummy just moved? I swear I saw its fingers twitch!"

"Don't be ridiculous," Jones scoffed, giving the sarcophagus a wide berth. "Though... do you think that movie, 'Night at the Museum,' might have been based on real events?"

"Oh god, I hope not," Martinez moaned. "I don't want to fight a T-Rex skeleton!"

We made it through several more rooms this way, Ginger and I barely containing our laughter at the guards' antics. In the Marine Life Room, Martinez nearly had a heart attack when he bumped into a hanging shark model, letting out a squeak that would have put a mouse to shame. Jones, meanwhile, kept eyeing the giant squid display suspiciously, as if expecting it to suddenly come to life and drag him into its glass case.

But our luck couldn't hold forever. As we entered the Ancient History Room, with its towering dinosaur skeletons, I realized with a sinking feeling that we'd run out of places to hide. The room was mostly open space, dominated by the massive ancient beasts.

Jones and Martinez entered right behind us, blocking our escape route. We ducked behind a massive dinosaur skeleton – a T-Rex. But I knew we were trapped. There was nowhere else to go unless we suddenly developed the ability to climb the dinosaur and perch on its skull.

Ginger looked up at me, his green eyes glinting in the darkness. "It's showtime," he meowed softly. "I'll lead them outside. Try not to get eaten by any resurrected dinosaurs while I'm gone."

Before I could stop him, he darted forward, emerging dramatically from inside the dinosaur skeleton. He let out a loud yowl that echoed through the room, causing both guards to jump in surprise. Martinez let out a yelp that sounded remarkably similar to Ginger's cry.

"Wait a minute," Jones said, squinting at Ginger. "Isn't that the same cat that caused a ruckus in the station last month? The one Murphy was chasing? The coffee-making feline?"

Martinez peered closer, his flashlight beam focused on Ginger. "It looks like Ginger, that detective cat. The one that works with Mr. Butterfield."

"It can't be," Jones protested. "Why would a respectable cat detective sneak into the museum at night? Unless... do you think Mr. Butterfield put him up to this?"

"Or maybe it's not him," Martinez mused. "These orange cats all look kind of similar. It could be some stray that snuck in looking for mice."

"Wait," Jones said slowly. "Does this mean the cat was playing disco music all along? Is this some kind of feline disco party we don't know about?"

Martinez shook his head, looking thoroughly confused. "I don't know, but we have to catch him. Miller ordered that there be no intruders on the crime scene. Even if they are musically inclined cats."

With that, they both took off after Ginger, who led them on a merry chase out of the Ancient History Room. I could barely contain my laughter as I watched Martinez nearly trip over his own feet in his eagerness to catch my feline partner. Jones wasn't faring much better, puffing and wheezing as he tried to keep up with Ginger's agile movements.

I waited until I heard the front door slam shut, then made my way quickly back to the security room. The museum felt different now – less ominous and more like the setting of some absurd comedy.

I opened the door to the security room, finding everyone inside looking tense and worried. The blue glow from the monitors cast an eerie light over their faces, making them look like characters in a sci-fi movie.

"It's time to go," I announced, trying to keep my voice steady despite the adrenaline still coursing through my veins.

Lily looked up, her eyes wide with concern. "Where's Ginger?"

"He'll join us later," I assured her. "We need to leave now."

I turned to Max. "Don't forget to delete the camera footage. We don't want to star in Miller's next training video on 'How Not to Secure a Crime Scene'."

Aaron chuckled, the sound tinged with nervous energy. "Yeah, we saw all that theatrics on the additional monitors in live format. The police would be quite entertained if they saw it. It was like watching a bizarre mix of 'Keystone Cops' and 'Cats: The Musical'."

Max nodded, his fingers flying over the keyboard with impressive speed. "I've deleted the last half hour of footage and turned off the cameras for the next 5 minutes. As far as the system is concerned, this has been the most boring night in museum history."

"Great," I said, ushering everyone toward the door. "Let's go then, before our luck runs out and Miller decides to make a surprise inspection."

We snuck out through the emergency exit, the cool night air a shock after the stuffy interior of the museum. Emma was waiting for us, pacing back and forth.

"I guess there was a need for Plan B after all," she said ruefully. "I tried everything to stop the guards. I even offered to do a full star chart reading for them. Usually, that keeps people occupied for hours!"

"It's not your fault," I assured her. "You did great. It's just that my daughter called and blew our cover. Apparently, the universe decided we needed an extra challenge tonight."

Ben looked at me, his brow furrowed in confusion. "Mr. Butterfield, don't you know how to turn on silent mode?"

I felt my face heat up, grateful for the darkness that hid my embarrassment. "I did turn it on before we left the house. At least, I thought I did."

Lily held out her hand. "Can I see your phone for a second?"

I handed it over, watching as she tapped through the settings with quick, confident touches. After a moment, she looked up, her expression full of amusement.

"You turned on power saving mode, not silent mode," she explained, handing the phone back to me.

I blinked, suddenly understanding why my phone seemed to discharge so rarely. "I always wondered about that," I muttered. "I thought I just had a really efficient battery."

Emma leaned in, her crystals jingling like a small orchestra. "Did you learn anything from the footage at least?"

I shook my head. "The footage from the Local Legends Room, where the protein bar was placed, was deleted by the thief." I turned to Max. "Did you check the other cameras while Ginger and I were performing our theatrics with the guards?"

Max nodded, his expression grim. "Same problem. Parts of the footage were deleted just when the thief could potentially move through the museum. It's like they knew exactly where every camera was. Either we're dealing with a professional, or the world's luckiest amateur."

Aaron sighed, running a hand through his hair. "So this whole breaking in was in vain? We risked arrest for nothing?"

"Not entirely," I countered, trying to inject some optimism into my voice. "At least we can confidently say it wasn't Ben who stole the egg. He was in the bathroom the whole time. So that's one suspect we can cross off our list."

"Great," Ben muttered. "I'm glad my gastrointestinal distress could contribute to the investigation."

Just then, Ginger came trotting around the corner, looking slightly ruffled but quite pleased with himself. His orange fur was sticking up in places, giving him the appearance of a feline punk rocker.

"And here comes the hero of the night," I announced, bending down to scratch behind his ears. I quickly explained to the others how he'd led the guards away so we could escape.

"Every cat could do it," Ginger meowed, though I could hear the pride in his voice. "Though I expect a premium salmon after my heroics. And maybe a medal. Do they give medals to cats for outstanding achievement in guard distraction?"

Lily scooped Ginger up, hugging him close. "Thank you, Ginger! You're amazing! The bravest cat detective in Oceanview Cove!"

Ginger preened under the attention, looking thoroughly pleased with himself. I could practically see his ego inflating like a balloon.

Everyone exchanged relieved glances, the tension of the night finally breaking. A few nervous chuckles escaped, quickly stifled as we remembered our proximity to the guards.

"Thank you all for this 'night expedition,'" I said, feeling a wave of gratitude for this motley crew. "I know it wasn't exactly how any of you planned to spend your evening."

Max grinned, his earlier worry replaced by excitement. "Are you kidding? It was thrilling! Way better than sitting at home watching reruns. I'd be up for it again if needed."

Emma nodded enthusiastically. "I'm always ready for things like this. The stars align perfectly for nocturnal adventures! Though next time, I'll bring some protective crystals. They're much more effective than trying to distract guards with impromptu astrology lessons."

Ben chuckled nervously, shifting from foot to foot. "Yeah, but I'd rather not play with fire again... or eat any more questionable protein bars, for that matter. I think I've had enough excitement to last me until next Easter. Or maybe the one after that."

We all exchanged knowing looks, the absurdity of the entire situation finally hitting us. Here we were, a mismatched group of amateur sleuths (and one very intelligent cat) who had just broken into a museum in the middle of the night, all to look at some security footage. It sounded like the plot of a low-budget crime comedy.

***

After bidding goodnight to our motley crew, Aaron, Lily, Ginger, and I began our walk home. The streets were quiet now, the only sound the distant lapping of waves against the shore and the occasional rustle of leaves in the gentle breeze.

Lily's face was thoughtful as we walked, her brow furrowed in concentration. "So we're definitely dealing with a tech genius who knows their way around not just drones, but security cameras too. This is absolutely like something out of a spy movie!"

I nodded, feeling the weight of the case settling back on my shoulders. "Right. And they've left almost no traces. We might have hit a dead end."

Aaron cleared his throat. "Jim, maybe you should call your daughter back, she might be worried. We can theorize later."

Lily nodded in agreement. "I'd be worried if my dad dismissed my calls like that. Even if he was in the middle of a top-secret museum break-in."

"You're right," I admitted, pulling out my phone. The screen glowed brightly in the darkness, momentarily blinding me.

I dialed Sarah's number, holding my breath as it rang. She picked up on the first ring, her voice a mix of relief and exasperation.

"Dad! What happened? Why did you dismiss all my calls?"

I winced at the concern in her voice. "I'm sorry, honey. I was just... busy. You know, it's already midnight. Shouldn't you be asleep?"

"Then why aren't you asleep?" she countered, her tone reminiscent of when she used to catch me sneaking late-night snacks. "I can hear the breeze outside. Are you not at home?"

I sighed, knowing I couldn't hide anything from her. Sarah had always been perceptive, even as a child. "Well, I was conducting a rather unorthodox nighttime investigation. The precious egg-"

"Was stolen," Sarah finished. "I know. That's why I was calling you. I found something that could help solve this case."

I blinked in surprise. "You did?"

"Yes," Sarah said, her voice picking up speed with excitement. "After putting the kids to bed, I was browsing the Oceanview Cove Gazette website and saw the article about the stolen egg. It reminded me of something I'd read a couple of months ago. So I dug deeper online and discovered multiple similar thefts along the East Coast over the past year or so. The pattern is always the same – a precious artifact gets stolen from a small coastal town museum."

I felt a chill run down my spine as the implications sank in. It seemed that the Easter Egg theft in Oceanview Cove might not have been just a random event, but part of a series of thefts.

Chapter 17

The night suddenly seemed much colder as I realized just how big this case might be. What had started as a simple egg theft was rapidly turning into something much larger and more complex. I exchanged a glance with Ginger, seeing my own concern reflected in his green eyes.

"Dad?" Sarah's voice came through the phone, pulling me back to the present. "Are you still there?"

"Yes, sorry," I said, shaking off my shock. "I'm just processing what you've told me. This is huge, Sarah. Can you send me links to all the articles you've found?"

"Of course," she replied. "I'll email them to you right away. But Dad... be careful, okay? If this is part of some larger operation, it could be dangerous."

I felt a surge of affection for my daughter. Even from miles away, she was still looking out for me. "I will, honey. Thank you for this information. It might be the breakthrough we needed."

After saying goodbye to Sarah, I turned to the others. Aaron and Lily were looking at me expectantly.

"Well?" Aaron prompted. "What did Sarah have to say?"

I took a deep breath, still trying to wrap my head around this new development. "It seems our little egg theft might be part of something much bigger. Sarah found reports of similar thefts in other small coastal towns along the East Coast over the past year."

Lily's eyes widened. "So it's not just a random theft? It's like... a professional operation?"

I nodded grimly. "That's what it looks like. Which means we're dealing with something far more complex than we initially thought."

"Well," Ginger meowed dryly, "I suppose we can kiss our quiet small-town life goodbye. Again. At this rate, we'll have to change the town's slogan to 'Oceanview Cove: Where Big City Crime Meets Coastal Charm'."

Ginger had a point. Our little town seemed to attract more than its fair share of criminal activity lately.

"What do we do now?" Lily asked, her voice a mix of excitement and apprehension.

I glanced at my watch, noting with surprise that it was well past midnight. "For now, we get some sleep. Tomorrow, we'll regroup and go over all the information we have. With this new perspective, we might see something we missed before."

Aaron nodded in agreement. "Good idea. It's been a long night, and we could all use some rest."

***

A persistent knocking jolted me from sleep. I squinted at the alarm clock on my nightstand, the glowing red numbers blurring into focus: 7:30 AM. Groaning, I buried my face deeper into the pillow. After our late-night museum adventure, I definitely hadn't gotten all the much-needed rest I'd hoped for.

The knocking continued, growing more insistent with each passing second. I heard Ginger stir from his spot on the windowsill, his tail swishing against the glass.

"You'd better open the door," he meowed, sounding far too alert for this ungodly hour. "What if it's the thief? Perhaps his conscience tormented him so much, he's decided to bring the egg back."

I snorted into my pillow. "Only that would justify such an early wake-up call," I muttered, finally forcing myself to sit up. I hastily pulled on a pair of sweatpants and an old t-shirt that had seen better days, then shuffled toward the door.

Stifling a yawn, I opened the door to find Aaron and Lily standing on my porch. Lily had small bags under her eyes, a clear sign of a sleepless night, but her expression was one of barely contained excitement. Aaron, on the other hand, looked slightly more refreshed, though there was a hint of resignation in his posture.

"What's this all about?" I asked, unable to keep the irritation from my voice. "I thought we'd meet later."

Aaron gave me an apologetic smile. "Lily woke me up too, but it's important. Just hear what she has to say."

I sighed, stepping back to let them in. "Alright, come in. But this better be worth the early wake-up call."

As we entered the living room, I saw Ginger already perched on the arm of my favorite armchair, his tail curled neatly around his paws. He fixed Lily and Aaron with an inquisitive look.

Lily practically bounced onto the couch, her enthusiasm apparently overriding any fatigue she might be feeling. Aaron settled next to her, looking both proud and slightly exasperated.

"I barely slept last night," Lily began, her words tumbling out in a rush. "I decided to investigate all those thefts further, and I found even more of them in Europe – Spain, Portugal, Italy, the list goes on!"

My gaze drifted to the coffee table, where yesterday's edition of the Oceanview Cove Gazette lay, its bold headlines proclaiming the latest local gossip. I couldn't help but think of Mrs. Henderson's wild theories, which suddenly didn't seem so wild anymore.

"So, it could be that Mrs. Henderson was right," I mused. "There are international art thieves indeed."

Lily nodded eagerly. "Seems like it, but the most curious thing is that all of these thefts happened only in coastal small towns."

My eyebrows shot up. "No towns deep into the mainland?"

"No, only coastal," Lily confirmed, pulling out her phone. "Here, let me show you."

She held out her phone, displaying a map dotted with what looked like dozens of tiny red pins along various coastlines. "I marked everywhere the thefts occurred," she explained.

I leaned in closer, my eyes widening as I took in the sheer number of dots. A strange feeling settled in the pit of my stomach as my gaze landed on the dot marking Oceanview Cove. Our little town, usually so removed from the world's larger dramas, was now part of what appeared to be an international crime spree.

"We have to make sure that Oceanview Cove's dot will be the last on this map," I said. "We need to catch the thief before they strike another town."

Lily nodded vigorously. "That's why I compiled a list of museums where the thefts occurred, along with their phone numbers. I thought we could call and ask for details about each theft. Maybe we'll see some clues or similarities to our case."

"Thank you, that's great work," I said, smiling despite my lingering fatigue. "It would have taken me at least a week to put together a list like that, considering my typing speed."

Aaron nodded, placing a hand on Lily's shoulder. "Yeah, Lily's talented when it comes to research. Though," he added, giving his daughter a pointed look, "sleep is also important. You should have done all this in the morning."

Lily had the grace to look slightly abashed. "I was just so excited to make a breakthrough in the case," she said, then quickly changed the subject. "So, when are we going to call the museums?"

I glanced at the clock on the wall. "It's not even 8 AM yet," I pointed out. "The museums are probably closed."

Ginger chose that moment to stretch languidly. "Perhaps we should start with a more pressing matter," he meowed. "Like breakfast. I'm sure even international art thieves need their morning coffee."

As if on cue, my stomach rumbled audibly. "You know what?" I said, addressing both Ginger and our guests. "Let me freshen up a bit. In the meantime, Ginger can make you some coffee."

Lily's eyes widened in surprise. "Ginger can make coffee?"

Her incredulous expression made me smile. "Unofficially, it's the best coffee in town."

"Officially, too," Ginger added, puffing out his chest with pride. Of course, only I could understand him, but his smug expression was universal.

Aaron looked between me and Ginger, clearly puzzled. "And how does he do that, exactly?"

I shrugged, already heading toward the bathroom. "I'm not entirely sure. He just presses some buttons on the coffee machine. Don't ask me how – I've learned not to question it."

***

By the time I emerged from the bathroom, feeling slightly more human and dressed in my usual detective attire of khaki pants and a sweater, the rich aroma of freshly brewed coffee had permeated the house. I found Aaron and Lily in the living room, both cradling steaming mugs and wearing expressions of pleasant surprise.

"You were right," Aaron said, raising his mug in a small salute. "This really is great coffee."

Ginger sat nearby, looking entirely too pleased with himself. His tail curled around his paws, and there was a distinct twinkle in his green eyes that seemed to say, "Of course it's great. I made it."

Lily took another sip, her eyes widening. "This is amazing! Ginger could work as a barista part-time."

Ginger's whiskers twitched at the suggestion. "I make coffee not for profit, but for the art of coffee-making," he meowed. "Besides, I have more important things to do – like keeping you all out of trouble."

"I need Ginger here to help solve cases," I said with a warm smile, settling into my armchair and reaching for the mug they'd thoughtfully set out for me.

As I took my first sip, I had to agree with Aaron and Lily – it was exceptional. How Ginger managed to coax such flavor out of my ancient coffee machine remained a mystery, but one I was happy to leave unsolved.

"So," I said, setting my mug down on the coffee table, "let's call those museums."

Just as I reached for Lily's list, my phone erupted in its familiar gospel rendition of "Stayin' Alive." I glanced at the screen.

"It's Robert," I announced, answering the call and putting it on speaker. "Good morning, Robert."

"Morning, Jim," Robert's voice filled the room. "Hope I didn't wake you."

"No, someone already did that earlier," I said, shooting a pointed look at Lily, who just grinned unrepentantly.

"Well, I'm calling about that fishing ship we discussed. It just docked."

I sat up straighter, suddenly alert. "Has anyone disembarked or boarded?"

"Not yet," Robert replied. "But I'll keep an eye out and call you if I see anything suspicious."

"Thanks, Robert," I said.

After ending the call, Aaron leaned forward, his expression thoughtful. "Maybe we should head down there and check out that ship ourselves."

I nodded, draining the last of my coffee. "We will, right after we make these calls to the museums. The more information we have, the better prepared we'll be."

Lily handed me her notepad, filled with neat rows of museum names and phone numbers. Her thorough work was remarkable.

Taking a deep breath, I dialed the first number, putting the call on speaker. The phone rang several times, and I was beginning to think no one would answer when a woman's voice finally came through.

"Hello, Bayside Historical Museum. How may I help you?"

"Good morning," I began, adopting my most professional tone. "My name is Jim Butterfield. I'm a private detective from Oceanview Cove, investigating a recent theft from our local museum. I understand your museum experienced a similar incident recently?"

There was a pause on the other end of the line, followed by a soft sigh. "Yes, that's correct," the woman replied, her voice tinged with sadness. "We still haven't caught the thief or recovered the artifact. I'm sorry to hear your town has fallen victim to a similar crime."

"I was hoping we could discuss some of the similarities," I pressed gently. "Any information could be helpful in our investigation."

Over the next few minutes, the woman described their theft in detail. The similarities were uncanny – the cut through the glass, the photographs covering cameras. The only difference was that they hadn't found any drone parts.

"Was there anything unusual about the day of the theft?" I asked. "Any staff members who acted out of character or weren't at their posts?"

The woman chuckled, though there was little humor in the sound. "Well, one of our security guards was indisposed for quite some time. Stomach trouble, apparently. He never saw the theft occur."

My eyebrows shot up. This was sounding more familiar by the second.

"And our janitor was the only one near the exhibit room when it happened," she continued. "But he didn't see or hear anything suspicious. Poor guy felt so guilty about it that he resigned shortly after."

That caught my attention. "He resigned? How long had he been working there?"

"Just about a month," the woman replied. "It was a shame to lose him so quickly. He'd told us he couldn't find work in the city, which is why he came to our little town. Such a nice, responsible young man."

A theory was beginning to form in my mind. "Let me guess," I said slowly. "Before coming to your museum, he was looking for work in the financial sector in the city?"

There was a startled pause on the other end of the line. "Yes, that's right. How did you know?"

"Just a hunch," I replied. "One last question – what was this janitor's name?"

The woman replied, "His name was Andrew Williams."

This was different from Josh Foster, though the other details matched closely.

"Thank you for your help," I said. "You've been incredibly helpful."

"Wait," the woman said quickly. "Do you suspect him of something? He seemed like such a nice young man."

I hesitated, not wanting to say too much. "I'd advise you to keep an eye on the news in the coming days," I said carefully. "There might be quite a story breaking soon."

After ending the call, I looked up to find Aaron and Lily staring at me with a mixture of confusion and anticipation.

"What was all that about?" Aaron asked.

I quickly explained what I'd learned from Dorothy about Josh – how he'd only been working at our museum for a month, how he'd come from the city after failing to find work in finance. The parallels were impossible to ignore.

Lily's eyes widened. "So it was Josh all along?"

"It's looking that way," I said grimly. "But let's call a few more museums to be sure."

Over the next twenty minutes, we called three more museums. Each time, the story was the same – a janitor arrives, works for about a month, a precious item gets stolen, and the janitor resigns. The only difference was the name used each time.

As I ended the final call, a heavy silence fell over the room.

"I guess we don't need to call the European museums," I said, rubbing my temples. "The situation seems pretty clear."

Lily shook her head, looking stunned. "I can't believe it was Josh. He seemed so helpful. He even brought the ladder so I could reach the camera."

Ginger, who had been quietly observing from his perch, let out a soft snort. "I knew from the very beginning there was something off about him," he meowed. "No one is that enthusiastic about cleaning museum floors."

Aaron leaned back, a look of grudging admiration on his face. "You have to admit, it's a genius scheme. Small town museums aren't as protected as those in big cities. Less security, budget constraints. And there aren't as many visitors. It's the perfect place to steal something valuable without drawing too much attention."

As Aaron spoke, a memory nagged at the back of my mind. "Lily," I said suddenly, "can you pull up that archive webpage of NautiluxTech's past employees?"

Lily nodded, her fingers flying over her phone's screen. Within seconds, she handed it to me. I studied the image of Aiden Wright, feeling a jolt of recognition.

"I knew I'd seen something familiar in Aiden Wright's eyes," I muttered, then held the phone out to Aaron and Lily. "Take another look at this. Who does it remind you of now?"

Lily gasped. "It's Josh!"

Aaron nodded slowly. "Just with a beard and a different hairstyle. And without the glasses."

"A master of disguise," Ginger commented dryly. "Though I suppose even criminal masterminds have to deal with changing fashion trends."

Before I could respond, my phone rang again. This time, it was Dorothy.

"Mr. Butterfield," Dorothy said as soon as I answered, her voice tight with worry. "You asked me to call if I noticed anything strange about the staff's behavior. Well, something has come up."

My attention sharpened immediately. "What is it, Dorothy?"

"It's Josh," she continued. "He just called and said he's resigning."

My heart skipped a beat. "Did he give a reason?"

"He said he blamed himself for the theft and couldn't handle it anymore," Dorothy replied. "I tried to reason with him, but he'd already made up his mind. He said he's leaving Oceanview Cove."

I could hear the sadness in her voice as she added, "Where will I find another janitor like him? He was so dedicated and efficient."

"I understand your concern, Dorothy," I said, trying to balance sympathy with the need to stay neutral. "It's always hard to lose a good employee. But I'm sure you'll find someone capable to fill the position. Thank you for letting me know about this."

As I ended the call, I turned to the others. "Josh – or should I say Aiden – isn't going on vacation like he told me earlier. He's trying to run away on that fishing ship with the stolen egg. And I'd bet my last dollar that Ethan Zhao is already on board, waiting to pick up his friend."

I stood up, feeling a surge of adrenaline. "We have to stop them."

Chapter 18

Lily's eyes shone with excitement as she looked between Aaron and me. "So, what's the plan?" she asked eagerly. "When do we head out to catch the thieves?"

Aaron's face hardened. "The plan is for you to stay right here while we try to stop that ship," he said firmly.

Lily's face fell, her earlier enthusiasm evaporating instantly. "No, I want to go too!" she protested. "Emma said I might play an important part in solving this. I want to help!"

I sighed, running a hand through my hair. "Emma predicts lots of things, Lily," I said gently. "You've already helped us a great deal, but you have to stay here. It could be dangerous out there, and we might not be as lucky as we were in the museum."

Lily opened her mouth to argue further, but Aaron cut her off with a stern look. "It's non-negotiable," he said, his voice leaving no room for debate. "Remember how worried I was during your island adventure last year? I can't go through that again."

The fight seemed to drain out of Lily as she slumped back against the couch cushions. "I guess you're right," she conceded reluctantly, though I could still see the disappointment in her eyes.

I felt a twinge of sympathy for her. It wasn't easy being left behind, especially when you knew you could contribute. But Aaron was right – the thieves' ship was no place for a teenager, no matter how clever she might be.

"Come on," I said to Aaron, already heading for the door. "We need to move fast if we're going to catch them."

Ginger trotted after us, his tail swishing with what I could only assume was anticipation. As we stepped out onto the porch, the morning air hit us with a refreshing coolness that belied the tension of the moment.

Aaron jingled his car keys. "Let's take my car," he suggested. "It'll be faster."

I nodded in agreement, thinking of my own ancient vehicle with a mixture of fondness and exasperation. "Good idea," I said. "By the time my car engine starts, Aiden and Ethan will already be halfway to Europe." I paused, a thought occurring to me. "Plus, I can make a couple of calls while you're driving."

As we made our way down the porch steps, a familiar voice called out to us. "Mr. Butterfield!"

I turned to see Mrs. Henderson on her own porch, phone pressed to her ear and an excited gleam in her eyes that I'd come to associate with fresh gossip. "I just received a call from my source at the town square," she announced, her voice carrying easily across the quiet street. "Josh is on the move with bags. He got into a taxi and is heading in the direction of the harbor."

I nodded, trying to keep my expression neutral. "Thank you, Mrs. Henderson," I called back, already moving toward Aaron's car.

But Mrs. Henderson wasn't finished. "Where's he going?" she pressed, her curiosity practically radiating off her in waves.

I shrugged, aiming for nonchalance. "Probably on a cruise," I replied, hoping the vague answer would satisfy her enough to avoid further questions.

No such luck. Mrs. Henderson's eyebrows shot up, her voice filled with disbelief. "On a cruise? Can janitors afford going on cruises these days?"

I pretended not to hear her last question, ducking into Aaron's car with what I hoped was a casual wave. As Aaron started the engine, I caught sight of Mrs. Henderson in the rearview mirror, phone still glued to her ear as she watched us drive away. No doubt the Oceanview Cove gossip network would be buzzing within minutes.

As we pulled away from the B&B, Ginger spoke up from the backseat. "I guess our morning run is off the table," he meowed.

I stifled a laugh, keeping my voice low so only Ginger could hear. "I predict we'll burn more calories now than during any morning run."

But Aaron, it seemed, had sharper ears than I'd given him credit for. "I hope we won't have to swim after the ship," he said, his knuckles whitening slightly on the steering wheel.

"It shouldn't come to that," I assured him, though a part of me wondered if I was trying to convince Aaron or myself.

Pushing aside my doubts, I pulled out my phone and dialed Robert. He picked up on the first ring, his voice tight with urgency. "Jim! I was just about to call you. A man just disembarked from the ship – looks like they really are refueling."

"We're heading to the docks now to stop that ship from sailing off," I told him quickly. "And Aiden... I mean, Josh Foster, is heading there too. We can't let him board that ship."

There was a pause on the other end of the line, then Robert's confused voice came through. "Josh Foster? The janitor from the museum?"

"Yes," I confirmed, realizing how bizarre it must sound. "He's the thief who stole the egg, and he's trying to run away on that ship now. I'll explain everything later, but for now, we need to stop him."

Robert's reply was immediate, despite his obvious bewilderment. "I'll do my best to stop him, but some help from the police wouldn't hurt. Even our local force would be better than nothing."

"You're right. I'll call them now."

Ending the call, I took a deep breath before dialing Sheriff Miller. This wasn't going to be an easy conversation.

Miller's voice, when he finally picked up, was gruff with irritation. "Butterfield, what's this about?"

I launched into a rapid-fire explanation, detailing the international art thief ring, Josh's true identity, and the imminent escape attempt. As I spoke, I could practically hear Miller's eyebrows rising higher and higher.

"Let me get this straight," he said when I finally paused for breath. "You're saying there are international art thieves involved in museum thefts over the past year, and one of them is a janitor from our museum?"

"I know how it sounds," I admitted, "but he's not just a janitor. He's a tech genius."

"And you're saying that he's trying to run away on the mysterious fishing ship that just docked in our harbor?"

"Exactly," I confirmed. "You have to send the whole police force to arrest these thieves."

There was a moment of silence, then Miller chuckled. The sound grated on my nerves. "Butterfield, you've outdone yourself this time. What a story!"

I gritted my teeth, fighting to keep my voice level. "Just go to the docks and check that ship for yourself," I insisted. "I'm sure you'll find there's a lot more than just fishing equipment on board."

Miller sighed. "Alright, I'll send Murphy there. That's the best I can do."

I closed my eyes briefly, disappointment washing over me. It wasn't the response I'd hoped for, but it was better than nothing. "Alright, thanks," I said, preparing to end the call.

"Wait," Miller's voice stopped me. "I got a report from Martinez and Jones that a cat that looks like yours snuck into the museum last night. Is that true?"

I froze. Keeping my voice as steady as possible, I replied, "I don't know anything about it. He was sleeping at home last night."

"Right," Miller said. "Those idiots probably confused everything again."

As I ended the call, Aaron glanced over at me. "Any progress?"

I shook my head, frustration evident in my voice. "None. The best he could do was to send Officer Murphy to the ship."

Aaron's lips thinned. "I didn't expect anything more than that."

From the backseat, Ginger let out a soft snort. "Ah yes, Officer Murphy. I'm sure our international art thieves are quaking in their boots now. Perhaps he can defeat them with the power of his incompetence alone."

I bit back a smile at Ginger's sarcasm, focusing instead on the road ahead. The docks were coming into view, and with them, the looming shape of the fishing vessel that had caused so much trouble.

As we drew closer, I could see that the ship, while not massive by ocean-going standards, dwarfed the other boats in our harbor. It looked out of place among the smaller fishing vessels and pleasure craft, like a wolf among sheep.

Aaron's voice broke through my thoughts. "Smart of them to dock at the far end," he observed. "Far from prying eyes."

I nodded in agreement, my gaze sweeping the area. That's when I noticed a taxi driving away from the far end of the docks.

Ginger, ever observant, spoke up. "The taxi is already driving away from there. It means that Aiden has arrived."

A knot of tension formed in my stomach. We were cutting it close.

Aaron parked the car a short distance from the ship, and we quickly piled out. As we approached on foot, I scanned the area, looking for any sign of Robert. The docks were eerily quiet, with no one visible near the mysterious vessel.

"Where's Robert?" I muttered, more to myself than to the others.

Aaron's voice was low, his eyes darting around warily. "Maybe he just saw the ship from afar and didn't get to it yet."

I looked toward the other end of the harbor, but there was no sign of our fisherman friend. Just other locals going about their morning routines, oblivious to the drama unfolding nearby.

"No," I said, a sinking feeling in my chest. "There's something wrong. Maybe he got to the ship late, when Aiden had already gone inside, and went after him."

Aaron's face set in determination. "We should board the ship while no one sees."

Ginger, padding silently beside us, let out a soft meow. "A great idea, going straight into the thieves' lair. What could possibly go wrong? Perhaps we'll stumble upon a secret underground lair while we're at it. Or better yet, a portal to another dimension where competent law enforcement actually exists."

I couldn't entirely disagree with Ginger's assessment. This was risky, but what choice did we have?

As we approached the gangplank, the sound of whistling drifted from the other side of the ship. Probably that man that Robert saw disembarking earlier for refuel, I thought. Pressing a finger to my lips, I signaled for silence.

We crept up the gangplank as quietly as we could, our footsteps muffled by the gentle lapping of waves against the hull. Just as we reached the deck, the sound of approaching footsteps sent us scrambling for cover. We barely managed to slip inside a nearby hallway as a crew member walked past, his gaze thankfully fixed on some point in the distance.

My heart was pounding so loudly I was sure the others could hear it. The narrow corridor we found ourselves in was dimly lit, with several doors leading off to what I assumed were cabins. From the far end, I could hear muffled voices.

We made our way down the hallway, every creak of the ship setting my nerves on edge. As we passed one of the cabins, I noticed the door was slightly ajar. Curiosity got the better of me, and I peered inside.

What I saw made my blood run cold.

The small room was filled with artifacts – precious items that I recognized from news reports of museum thefts. And there, nestled among them like some twisted trophy, was our stolen Easter egg.

But it was the figure on the floor that made my heart stop. Robert lay motionless, his face pale in the dim light.

Aaron, noticing my shock, looked in as well. He quickly checked Robert's pulse, his voice barely above a whisper as he reported, "He's alive. No visible injuries. They probably tased him."

Anger surged through me, hot and fierce. "They're going to jail," I growled softly, my fists clenching at my sides. Taking a deep breath to calm myself, I added, "Let's hear what those two at the end of the corridor are talking about."

We crept further down the hallway, coming to a stop outside the last cabin. The door was partially open, allowing the whole conversation to be heard clearly. Carefully, I peered inside.

Two men stood in the small cabin, deep in conversation. One I recognized immediately as Josh Foster – or rather,

Aiden Wright. The other was unmistakably Ethan Zhao, looking almost exactly as he did in the photo from the article.

"So how did the theft go?" Ethan asked, his tone casual as if inquiring about a mundane errand.

Aiden's voice was filled with pride as he replied, "Smooth as silk. Perfect timing, cameras covered, footage deleted. Only hiccup was a piece of the drone falling off. Got those local detectives sniffing around more than I'd like."

Ethan's voice sharpened. "A piece fell off? How'd that happen?"

"Yeah," Aiden confirmed, sounding slightly defensive. "When I was closing the vent. Those old things are trickier than they look." He paused, then added reassuringly, "Don't worry, we've got plenty of spare parts, and I'm sure those detectives didn't suspect a thing. I played my part well."

There was a moment of silence, then Ethan spoke again, his voice lower. "And yet, that nosy fisherman tried to stop you from getting on board."

Aiden's laugh was cold. "Don't know what got into him. Maybe the sun fried his brain." There was a pause, and I could almost hear the smirk in his voice as he added, "A little shock from the taser cooled him down pretty quick though."

"So what are we going to do with him?" Ethan asked, a note of concern in his voice. "He'll definitely report it to the police and they'll be on our tail."

Aiden's response was chilling in its casualness. "We'll take him with us and throw him overboard on our way to the next town."

I felt sick to my stomach. These weren't just thieves – they were cold-blooded killers in the making. We had to stop them, and fast.

But before I could signal to Aaron that we needed to act, a gruff voice behind us made my heart skip a beat.

"Who are you?"

In my panic, I lost my footing. My feet tangled beneath me, and I crashed to the floor, bringing Aaron down with me. We tumbled unceremoniously into the cabin, landing in an undignified heap at the feet of the very men we'd been eavesdropping on.

Aiden's eyes widened in shock as he took in the scene before him. For a moment, he looked genuinely surprised. Then, as he assessed us and likely concluded we posed little threat, his composure returned. A slow, calculating smile spread across his face.

"Well, well, well," he said, his voice dripping with false cheerfulness. "What do we have here?"

Chapter 19

The cabin suddenly felt much smaller, the walls closing in around us as the gravity of our situation sank in. The ship's gentle rocking, barely noticeable before, now felt like a taunt.

Ethan, his face a mask of confusion, turned to Aiden. "Who are they? Do you know them?"

Aiden's eyes never left us as he answered, "It's that local detective I was talking about, though I don't see his feline partner."

At the mention of Ginger, I felt a surge of panic. I looked around frantically, my heart sinking as I realized he was nowhere to be seen.

The gruff man who had caught us – a burly sailor – spoke up, his voice as rough as sandpaper. "The cat just ran past me," he grunted. "Maybe got scared."

I felt a flicker of hope. Knowing Ginger, there was no way he'd simply run away. He had to be up to something.

Aiden's laugh cut through my thoughts, sharp and mocking. "Guess your furry sidekick cut and run," he sneered. Then his gaze shifted to Aaron. "And here's another detective in the making, though his daughter is also not here." His eyes narrowed suspiciously. "She skulking around the ship somewhere?"

Aaron's face remained impassive as he answered vaguely, "She's where she needs to be, Josh. Or should I say, Aiden?"

The surprise that flashed across Aiden's face was impossible to miss. His composure cracked, just for a moment, but it was enough. I seized the opportunity, my voice steady despite the fear churning in my gut.

"That's right, Aiden Wright and Ethan Zhao," I said, meeting their eyes. "We know everything about your little thieves' ring and about the other thefts in coastal town museums."

The atmosphere in the cabin shifted, tension crackling like electricity. Ethan's face darkened as he turned to Aiden. "You said that no one suspected a thing," he hissed. "How come they know everything about us?"

Aiden waved dismissively, but I could see the tension in his shoulders. "Don't worry," he said. "It's not like they're going anywhere. We'll deal with them the same way we'll deal with Robert."

A chill ran through me at the casual mention of Robert. As Aiden reached for his taser, panic gripped me. I needed to buy time, to keep them talking until... until what? Until Ginger's mysterious plan unfolded? Until help arrived? I wasn't sure, but I knew we needed more time.

"Wait!" I blurted out, my voice echoing in the small cabin. "Don't you want to know how we learned everything about you? So you don't make the same mistakes in the future?"

Ethan grabbed Aiden's arm, stopping him. "Let's hear what they have to say," he said, curiosity warring with caution in his eyes.

Aiden hesitated, then reluctantly tucked the taser away. "Fine," he growled. "Start talking."

I tried to stand up, my muscles protesting after our ungraceful tumble, but Aiden's sharp voice stopped me. "Stay right where you are," he snapped. "No sudden movements."

Sighing, I settled back onto the uncomfortable floor. The floor was rock-hard, and every roll of the ship sent aches through my body. The air in the cabin was thick with tension and the faint smell of fish – a reminder that this was, ostensibly, a fishing vessel.

"It all started with that drone part we found in the vent," I began, watching their faces carefully. "I saw Victor Sterling's company name etched on it and went straight to Victor in jail to question him about it. He told me everything about the spider drone prototype and about two talented engineers who were involved in creating these drones."

I paused, gauging their reactions. Aiden's face was a mask of indifference, but I could see the tightness around his eyes. Ethan, on the other hand, looked genuinely interested.

"Though," I continued, "Victor said that you were supposed to sell those drones on the black market. How come you still have them?"

Aiden chuckled, the sound devoid of any real humor. "Victor," he said, shaking his head. "He always had a big mouth, but he never really knew what was going on in his own company. That's why his company went bankrupt, and that's why we were able to keep one of the drones for ourselves without him knowing."

"But Victor said that selling the drones fetched a tidy sum," I pressed, sensing we were getting closer to the truth.

Ethan stepped forward, his eyes gleaming with a hint of pride. "We raised the price for the other drones," he explained, "but kept one of them for ourselves. We wanted to sell it later for a higher price."

Aiden picked up the thread, his voice taking on an almost boastful tone. "But then I got a better idea of how to use it to make even more money and told it to Ethan."

As they spoke, I was struck by the audacity of their plan. The complexity of it all – the drones, the museum thefts, the fishing vessel cover – it was like something out of a Hollywood heist movie. And yet, here we were, caught in the middle of it in our sleepy coastal town.

Ethan continued, a hint of wistfulness in his voice. "I had a passion for the ocean and wanted to become a sailor after we were fired from Victor's company. Then I thought, hey, why not combine that with making some serious cash?"

"The idea was genius," Aiden added, his eyes shining with a fervor that was almost unsettling. "I steal a precious artifact from the museum in a small coastal town, and then Ethan and his crew pick me up from the docks. No one would suspect a thing."

"Until now," Ethan said, his voice hardening. "If it weren't for that storm, we would've picked Aiden up the day of the theft and avoided all this trouble." He turned to me, eyes narrowing. "You said earlier that you recognized the company name on the drone part. Where else did you see other such drones?"

I took a deep breath, knowing that what I was about to say could potentially escalate the situation. "At the boat racing tournament last month," I said carefully. "Drones from Victor's company were used to sabotage some competitors' boats. They helped a racer named Marcus win."

The mention of Marcus's name sent a ripple of tension through the room. I pressed on, knowing I was treading on dangerous ground. "It's a complicated story, but we suspected that Marcus had an accomplice who actually navigated those drones from the shore during the race." I fixed my gaze on Aiden. "That accomplice was you, right?"

A slow, satisfied grin spread across Aiden's face, while Ethan looked at him with surprise. The tension in the room ratcheted up another notch.

Aiden leaned back against the wall, his posture relaxed but his eyes sharp. "I met Marcus when I had just settled in this town a month ago," he began, his voice taking on a storyteller's cadence. "We bumped into each other at Rose's café. Marcus was in Oceanview Cove to scope out the local waters for the boat race."

He paused, a smirk playing at the corners of his mouth. "We got to talking. He figured out I wasn't local and didn't care about the town's racers, so he let me in on Victor's plan. Offered me a cut of the prize money if I helped him win the race."

Aiden shrugged, as if discussing a perfectly normal business transaction. "I thought – why not? I'd get to make some money and also get a chance to check out the drones Victor's company was making. Well, I didn't end up getting any money because Marcus got killed, unfortunately, but at least I got to examine the drones. Still impressive engineering. It's a shame the company went bankrupt."

As Aiden spoke, I felt a wave of disgust and astonishment wash over me. The casual way he discussed manipulating the race, potentially ruining lives and dreams, was chilling.

Ethan looked at Aiden, a hint of amusement in his eyes. "Sounds like you had fun in this town."

Aiden's response was casual, almost flippant. "Yeah, this place was definitely less of a snooze fest than the others."

Then Ethan's expression turned serious as he faced me again. "Alright, let's get back to your story, detective. What happened next after you learned about the drones?"

I took a moment to gather my thoughts, then began recounting our investigation.

"We pieced together several clues," I explained. "First, we found Victor's company archive webpage, which had profiles of Aiden Wright and Ethan Zhao. Then we heard about a mysterious ship heading to our harbor. Finally, we stumbled across an article praising a heroic sailor named Ethan Zhao, complete with a photo."

I paused, studying their reactions. Ethan's face remained impassive, but I caught a flicker of something – pride, perhaps? – in his eyes at the mention of the article.

"We found your number on the sailors' forum and tried to call," I continued. "Why didn't you pick up?"

Ethan shrugged, his voice nonchalant. "That's just my backup phone now. Hardly ever check it." He frowned slightly. "Guess I should take down that comment on the forum."

"Then we called other museums where thefts had occurred," I said. "The details were identical. That's when we connected all the dots."

As I finished speaking, a heavy silence fell over the cabin. The gravity of the situation seemed to press down on us all, the air thick with unspoken tensions and calculations.

Aaron, who had been quietly observing, finally spoke up. His voice was calm, but I could hear the underlying strain. "I still don't get it. Why go through all that trouble with the photos, the cleaning sign, deleting footage? Couldn't you have just sent the drone through the vent and grabbed the egg?"

Aiden's response was quick, his tone dripping with condescension. "It's called being careful," he explained, as if talking to a particularly slow child. "If I hadn't done all that, someone could've walked in, or Max might've spotted something on the cameras. Then the whole thing would've gone up in smoke."

Ethan nodded, backing up his partner. "That kind of attention to detail is why we've pulled off so many jobs without a hitch."

Their words hung in the air, a testament to the meticulous planning that had gone into each of their crimes. It was chilling to think about how many times they had successfully pulled off this scheme.

A question had been nagging at me, so I decided to voice it. "Why not just do it at night? You had keys to every door in the museum anyway."

Ethan and Aiden exchanged a look, and to my surprise, Aiden's face reddened slightly. The sudden change in his demeanor was so unexpected that I found myself leaning forward, intrigued.

Aiden cleared his throat, clearly uncomfortable. "It's because of that movie, 'Night at the Museum'."

Aaron and I exchanged confused glances. Of all the possible explanations, this was the last one I'd expected.

Aiden continued, his words tumbling out. "I saw it as a kid, and ever since, I've been freaked out about being in museums at night."

I couldn't believe my ears. The thief who'd stolen so many artifacts from museums was afraid of being in them after dark? It seemed too ridiculous to be true.

Aaron let out a short laugh, disbelief evident in his voice. "What, you think the dinosaurs are gonna come to life?"

Aiden's face remained serious, his cheeks still flushed with embarrassment. He didn't respond, but his silence spoke volumes.

Ethan stepped in, his voice calm and matter-of-fact. "It's true," he confirmed. "That's why we had to plan everything so carefully."

He continued. "Out of the two of us who know the drones inside and out, only Aiden had the guts to actually commit the thefts. I'm more of a relaxed person, which is why I'd rather play the role of some kind of water taxi."

As Ethan spoke, I couldn't help but marvel at the strange turns life could take. Here we were, in the belly of a fishing vessel turned getaway boat, listening to international art thieves discuss their methods and motivations. And one of them was afraid of museums at night because of a children's movie. If I hadn't been living it, I wouldn't have believed it.

"Do the other crew members know about all of this?" I asked, curiosity getting the better of me.

Ethan nodded. "Of course. They'll also get a cut when we sell all of those artifacts on the black market."

Aiden, his face still red but his composure somewhat regained, cut in. "Okay, storytime's over," he snapped. "Let's blow this joint."

No sooner had the words left Aiden's mouth, a commotion erupted on the docks. The sound of a growing crowd filtered through the cabin walls, voices raised in what sounded like a mix of anger and excitement.

Someone's voice crackled over a radio, urgency clear in their tone. "Ethan, you have to see this."

Ethan moved to the window, his expression shifting from annoyance to alarm. He turned to Aiden, his voice tight. "Looks like the whole town's in on it now, not just these detectives. This is exactly why I said we need real guns, not these taser toys – for situations like this."

Aiden joined him at the window, his eyes widening in shock.

Ethan barked an order into the radio. "Wrap up the refueling, get back on board. We're setting sail."

I desperately wanted to see what was happening outside, but I feared that if I moved, I'd end up on the wrong end of Aiden's taser. So I remained still, my mind racing with possibilities. What had caused such a commotion? And more importantly, how could we use it to our advantage?

Ethan's voice cut through my thoughts as he issued another order through the radio. "Fire up the engine. We're leaving now."

There was a crackle of static, then a hesitant voice replied. "Uh, we've got a problem. Some cat just ran through here, dumped coffee all over the control panel. The electronics are fried. We can't start the engine."

Ethan's face contorted with anger. "A cat? Are you kidding me?"

Aiden smacked his forehead, realization dawning. "Ginger," he growled.

A surge of pride and relief washed over me. A grin spread across my face. In that moment, I had never been happier to have a feline partner.

Ethan's voice was tight with barely controlled rage as he spoke into the radio again. "Wait right there. I'm coming." He turned to the gruff man who had caught us earlier. "Come with me," he ordered. As he strode out of the room, he called back to Aiden, "Keep an eye on these two."

But Aiden wasn't listening. His attention was fixed on something outside the window, his expression a mix of fascination and disbelief.

In that moment of distraction, Aaron sprang into action. With surprising agility, he leapt to his feet, his hand darting into Aiden's pocket and emerging with the taser. Before Aiden could react, Aaron pressed the device against him and activated it.

Aiden's body went rigid, a strangled gasp escaping his lips before he crumpled to the floor, unconscious.

I struggled to my feet, wincing as my stiff joints protested. "Wow," I said, impressed. "I didn't know you could move like that."

Aaron barely acknowledged my comment. His attention was fixed on whatever was happening outside. "Jim," he said urgently. "You need to see this."

I joined him at the window, my jaw dropping at the scene before me.

"Now I get why Ethan wanted guns," I said, shaking my head in amazement. "They are about to learn why you don't mess with Oceanview Cove."

Chapter 20

The scene outside the ship's window was unlike anything I'd ever witnessed in Oceanview Cove. What seemed like half the town's population had gathered on the docks, armed with an assortment of makeshift weapons that looked more suited for a community theater production than an actual standoff. Baseball bats, rolling pins, and even what appeared to be a particularly menacing-looking garden gnome were clutched in determined hands.

In the midst of this unlikely militia, I spotted familiar faces. Shawn, his usual bartender's apron replaced by a determined expression and a wooden spoon that he brandished like a sword. Emma, her crystals glinting in the sunlight as she waved what looked suspiciously like a crystal-encrusted spatula. Chuck, wielding his trusty mop with the air of a warrior about to charge into battle. Sophie and Alice stood side by side, armed with rolling pins that still had traces of flour on them.

Max and Ben were there too, looking slightly sheepish but no less determined. Max clutched a flashlight like it was a lightsaber, while Ben had opted for a more practical approach with a fire extinguisher. I wondered if he was planning to blind the thieves with foam or just knock them out with the canister itself.

But what truly caught my eye was the figure standing at the forefront of this motley crew. Mrs. Henderson stood proud and tall, with what I now realized was the heavy machine gun I'd seen listed in the firearm database set up on the ground before her, ready to use. The weapon gleamed in the sunlight, looking comically out of place next to her frail form but finally answering the question of why on earth she owned such a thing.

And next to her, to my utter disbelief, stood Lily.

Aaron's sharp intake of breath told me he'd spotted her too. "I told her to stay at your house," he muttered, his voice a mix of exasperation and grudging admiration.

"Looks like she took matters into her own hands," I replied. "Something tells me she and Mrs. Henderson are the masterminds behind this little uprising. We should probably be grateful."

As if on cue, Mrs. Henderson's voice crackled through a megaphone, the sound slightly distorted but no less commanding. "Attention, international art thieves!" she bellowed. "We demand that you surrender and free the hostages immediately, or we will be forced to take action!"

The absurdity of the situation wasn't lost on me. Here we were, witnesses to what could only be described as the world's most bizarre standoff, with a retired librarian and a teenager facing off against international criminals.

A familiar meow drew my attention away from the window. I turned to see Ginger sauntering into the room, his tail held high and his whiskers twitching with what could only be described as feline smugness.

"Ah, our hero arrives," I said, unable to keep the grin off my face. "If it weren't for you, we'd probably be feeding the sharks somewhere in the middle of the ocean by now."

Ginger looked pleased with himself, his chest puffing out slightly at the praise. He leapt gracefully onto the windowsill, peering out at the scene below. "I see I haven't missed the main event," he meowed.

Aaron seemed too preoccupied with Lily's presence to pay much attention to the cat. His eyes never left his daughter as he mumbled, "Good job, Ginger," almost absentmindedly.

The scene outside was rapidly evolving into something that could only be described as organized chaos. The townsfolk, emboldened by Mrs. Henderson's rallying cry, began to advance toward the ship. Chuck led the charge, his mop raised high like a knight's lance in some bizarre medieval reenactment gone horribly wrong.

"For Oceanview Cove!" he bellowed, his voice cracking slightly on the high note.

The rest of the crowd took up the cry, though their battle slogans left something to be desired in terms of intimidation.

"You mess with our egg, you get the rolling pin!" Sophie yelled, brandishing her baking implement like a sword.

"The stars have aligned against you, evildoers!" Emma chimed in, her crystals creating a dazzling light show as she waved her spatula.

Even Ben got into the spirit, shouting something about "facing the foam of justice" as he awkwardly hefted his fire extinguisher.

"This has got to be the most ridiculous thing I've ever seen," I muttered to Ginger.

"Oh, I don't know," Ginger replied, his tail swishing with amusement. "I'd say it's neck and neck with your attempts at using a smartphone."

Just as the situation seemed poised to descend into complete absurdity, the wail of police sirens cut through the air. A convoy of police cars appeared at the edge of the docks, lights flashing and sirens blaring. They screeched to a halt near the crowd, and out stepped Sheriff Miller, followed by what looked like every available officer in the town.

"Well, well," I said, unable to keep the surprise out of my voice. "Looks like Miller finally decided to join the party."

Miller, his face a curious mix of determination and utter bewilderment, strode through the crowd. The sea of improvised weapons parted before him, though I noticed more than a few disappointed looks from those who'd clearly been itching for some action.

He reached Mrs. Henderson, who reluctantly relinquished the megaphone. Miller cleared his throat, his voice booming across the docks with all the authority his position could muster.

"This is the police!" he announced, as if that wasn't abundantly clear from the sea of uniforms behind him. "We have you surrounded! Come out with your hands up!"

I rolled my eyes. "Really? That's the best he could come up with? I've heard more original lines in a B-movie."

Ginger snorted, a sound that somehow managed to convey both amusement and disdain. "Well, what did you expect? 'Attention, art thieves, please exit the vessel in an orderly fashion and form a queue for arrest'?"

Despite the absurdity of the situation, I couldn't help but feel a surge of pride for our little town. They might not be the most coordinated or well-equipped militia, but they'd shown up when it counted. Even if their methods were... unconventional, to say the least.

Inside the ship, the atmosphere had shifted dramatically. Ethan burst back into the room, his face a mask of panic. "We're surrounded," he gasped, his earlier bravado completely evaporated. His eyes darted to Aiden's unconscious form on the floor, then to the taser in Aaron's hand. "And this idiot couldn't even watch over two men lying on the floor! Now because of him, there's a whole army out there!"

I couldn't resist. "Not an army," I corrected, unable to keep the smirk off my face. "Just a very determined group of small-town citizens who don't appreciate having their artifacts stolen. Oh, and the police. Can't forget them, even if they are fashionably late to the party."

Ethan's face cycled through a range of emotions – disbelief, anger, and finally, resignation. He slumped against the wall, the fight going out of him. "This is insane," he muttered. "We've pulled off heists in museums on two continents, and we're being taken down by a bunch of angry townspeople with kitchen utensils?"

"Don't forget the cat," Aaron chimed in, gesturing toward Ginger. "He's the one who really threw a wrench in your plans. Or should I say, a coffee pot?"

Ginger preened at the acknowledgment, his tail curling with satisfaction. "Finally, the recognition I deserve," he meowed. "Though I must say, dousing their control panel in coffee was far too mundane for my tastes. Next time, I'll have to come up with something more creative. Perhaps reprogramming their navigation system to lead them straight to the nearest coast guard station?"

I bit back a laugh, focusing instead on the scene unfolding outside. Miller had taken charge, directing his officers to secure the perimeter of the ship. The townsfolk, seemingly satisfied that the situation was under control, had started to mill about, their makeshift weapons lowered but not abandoned.

"I think it's time we made our grand exit," I said to Aaron. "Let's wake Robert up and get out of here before Miller decides we need to be arrested too, just for good measure."

Aaron nodded, and we quickly made our way back to the cabin where we had seen Robert earlier. He was still unconscious. Together, we managed to rouse him, his eyes blinking open in confusion.

"Wha... what happened?" Robert mumbled, wincing as he tried to sit up. "Last thing I remember, I was trying to stop Josh from boarding the ship, and then... nothing."

"Long story short," I said, helping him to his feet, "you got tased, we nearly got kidnapped, Ginger saved the day with some creative use of coffee, and now half the town is outside ready to storm the ship with kitchen utensils. Just another day in Oceanview Cove, really."

Robert blinked, clearly trying to process this information. "Right," he said slowly. "And I suppose next you'll tell me Mrs. Henderson is out there with her machine gun?"

Aaron and I exchanged glances. "Well..." Aaron began.

Robert's eyes widened. "You're kidding."

"I wish I was," I replied, unable to keep the amusement out of my voice. "Come on, let's get you out of here. I think you might need to see this to believe it."

The bright sunlight was almost blinding after the dim interior of the ship. As our eyes adjusted, we were greeted by a cacophony of cheers and applause. The crowd surged forward, their earlier battle-ready expressions replaced by looks of relief and excitement.

Mrs. Henderson's voice rose above the din. "I told you all!" she crowed. "Didn't I say there were international art thieves at work? Barbara's cousin in Maine told me about similar thefts – it was all connected! You'll read all about it in my book!"

I marveled at Mrs. Henderson's tenacity. Even now, with the case solved and the thieves apprehended, she was already thinking about how to spin this into her next bestseller.

My attention was drawn to Lily, who was now engulfed in her father's protective embrace. Aaron's arm was draped over her shoulders, his relief at having her safe palpable.

"So," I said, raising an eyebrow at Lily, "I take it this whole town militia thing was your idea?"

Lily grinned, her eyes sparkling with a mix of mischief and pride. "Well, I knew I couldn't do anything alone," she explained. "So I thought, why not use Mrs. Henderson's gossip network for good? I approached her at her porch down the street, explained the whole situation about the art thieves and the egg, and within ten minutes, half the town knew what was going on."

I had to admit, I was impressed. "Quick thinking," I praised. "Though I'm sure your dad would have preferred if you'd stayed put like he asked."

Aaron's grip on Lily's shoulder tightened slightly. "We'll be having a long talk about following instructions later," he said, though the pride in his voice somewhat undercut the sternness of his words.

"Oh!" Lily exclaimed, her eyes widening as if she'd just remembered something. "I also might have sent an anonymous tip to Sheriff Miller's email. You know, just in case Mrs. Henderson's network wasn't enough."

I blinked in surprise, then burst out laughing. "Well, that explains the cavalry's timely arrival," I said, glancing over to where Miller was overseeing the arrest of Ethan, Aiden, and their crew.

Miller, seeming to sense my gaze, looked up. Our eyes met, and for a moment, I saw a flicker of grudging respect in his expression. It was quickly replaced by his usual gruff demeanor, but the message was clear – he knew we'd been right all along.

Emma's excited voice cut through the crowd. "You see?" she exclaimed. "It all turned out exactly as I predicted! Lily played a crucial role, just like the stars foretold!"

Lily's grin widened at this. Whether it was celestial alignment or just good old-fashioned detective work (with a healthy dose of teenage ingenuity), we'd managed to crack the case and catch a ring of international art thieves.

Shawn's voice rose above the general hubbub. "I say this calls for a celebration!" he announced. "Everyone's invited to the Salty Breeze tonight. It's not every day we get to toast the downfall of international art thieves!"

A cheer went up from the crowd. It seemed that Oceanview Cove was more than ready to turn this bizarre day into a full-fledged party.

As the excitement began to die down and people started to disperse, I felt a wave of exhaustion wash over me. It had been a long, strange morning, and it wasn't over yet.

"I need to call Sarah," I said to no one in particular. "She's not going to believe what kind of case she helped us solve."

***

The Salty Breeze was alive with excitement that evening. The usual cozy atmosphere had been transformed into something more festive, with colorful streamers adorning the walls and a hand-painted banner proclaiming "Congratulations to Oceanview Cove's Finest Detectives!" hanging behind the bar.

I settled into a seat at the table near the bar, Ginger perched regally on the chair next to me. Aaron and Lily sat across from us, with Emma claiming the seat to my left. Shawn bustled back and forth, somehow managing to both serve drinks and participate in the animated conversations erupting all around the bar.

My fingers curled around the cool glass of my Librarian cocktail, its familiar taste a comforting presence after the day's excitement. Ginger lapped contentedly at a saucer of cream, while Lily sipped on something fruity and non-alcoholic that Shawn had concocted especially for her.

"I still can't believe it," Aaron said, shaking his head in amazement. "When we came here for a quiet Easter celebration, I never imagined we'd end up in the middle of an international art heist."

Lily's eyes sparkled with excitement. "It was amazing, wasn't it? The way everything came together, how we all worked as a team to solve the case and catch the thieves!"

I nodded, taking a sip of my drink. "You both were instrumental in cracking this case," I said. "Lily, your research skills and quick thinking were invaluable. And Aaron, that move with the taser? Impressive doesn't begin to cover it."

"It was nothing special," he said, though I could see a hint of pride in his eyes. "Just a lucky shot, really."

"Lucky or not," I replied, "it was exactly what we needed at that moment. You two make quite the detective duo."

Aaron glanced at Lily, a soft smile playing on his lips. "You know," he said thoughtfully, "maybe we should visit Oceanview Cove more often. There's certainly never a dull moment here."

Ginger, who had been quietly lapping at his cream, looked up at this. "Oh yes," he meowed sarcastically, "because what every vacation needs is a side of murder, poisoning, and grand larceny. Perhaps next time we can arrange for a nice kidnapping or maybe a spot of arson, just to keep things interesting."

I suppressed a smile, instead saying to Aaron, "We'd love to have you visit more often. Though I can't promise every trip will be quite this exciting."

"Or dangerous," Lily added with a grin.

At that moment, Robert joined our table, sliding into an empty chair with a groan. "Sorry I'm late," he said, accepting a beer from Shawn with a grateful nod. "The doctors at the hospital were insistent on running every test known to man before they'd let me leave. I told them I was fine, but apparently being tased is cause for concern."

"Can't imagine why," I quipped. "It's not like you were hit with enough electricity to power a small town or anything."

Robert chuckled, wincing slightly as he shifted in his seat. "Well, I wasn't about to miss this gathering. It's not every day we catch international art thieves in our little town."

Emma tilted her head thoughtfully. "You know, I wonder why all these crimes seem to happen on holidays or celebrations," she mused. "I should examine my star charts, see if there's a cosmic pattern we're missing."

Shawn, who had joined our table during a lull in drink orders, grinned. "Well, at least there's no major holidays coming up for the next couple of months. Maybe we'll finally get a bit of peace and quiet around here."

As soon as the words left Shawn's mouth, I felt a sense of foreboding wash over me. In Oceanview Cove, saying things like that was practically asking for trouble.

Ginger, who had been contentedly grooming himself after finishing his cream, looked up. "Oh, by the way," he meowed casually, "my birthday is next month. At least, that's when Peter and I always celebrated it."

I blinked in surprise, this information completely new to me. I had no idea Ginger even had a designated birthday, let alone when it was.

Bending down as if to scratch behind Ginger's ears, I whispered, "Don't worry, we'll organize an unforgettable birthday party for you. But let's keep it quiet for now, okay? I'd rather not tempt fate and end up with another mystery on our hands during your special day."

Ginger paused in his grooming, fixing me with a look that was equal parts amusement and exasperation. "Please," he meowed softly, "as if I'd let a little thing like a murder or a theft interrupt my birthday celebrations. I plan to enjoy my day to the fullest, mystery-free. Though knowing this town, we'll probably end up solving the case of the missing cake or the great catnip caper."

I shook my head, a wry smile playing on my lips. "Let's hope not," I murmured. "For once, I'd like to attend a celebration that doesn't end with handcuffs and police sirens."

The End
... of the seventh book in the series

Jim and Ginger's Next Case

Jim and Ginger return in *"Birthday Murder"* where they take on the case of a guest murdered in Jim's bedroom during Ginger's birthday party.

https://mybook.to/BirthdayMurder

Bonus Content

Get a FREE Jim and Ginger story!

Enjoy "The Curious Case of the Creeping Hedge" – an exclusive short story not available anywhere else!

Subscribe to Arthur Pearce's newsletter today and receive:

- Your free short story
- Updates on new releases
- Special discounts and cover reveals

https://www.arthurpearce.com/newsletter

Jim and Ginger's First Case

New to the series? Start with *"Murder Next Door"* where Jim and Ginger take on their first case when a friendly neighbor turns up dead.

https://mybook.to/MurderNextDoor

Printed in Great Britain
by Amazon